With a burning blush in her cheek but a proud smile on her lips, the young woman surveyed the crowd.

She was tall, with dark, flowing hair that gleamed in the sunlight. Her rich complexion highlighted her deep black eyes. . . . But it was the Scarlet Letter, embroidered with such extravagance on her dress, that caught the eye of everyone in the crowd. . . .

"We should tear that letter from her dress," muttered the eldest of the hags in the group, "and carve the A into her fair flesh! That would be more fitting punishment."

"Hush, my friends!" whispered the youngest woman in the group. "I'll guarantee that every stitch in that letter she has felt in her heart."

The grim jailer now made a gesture with his staff. . . .

The crowd of spectators fell back. Preceded by the jailer, Hester Prynne walked through the crowd toward the place appointed for her punishment.

A Background Note about *The Scarlet Letter*

The Scarlet Letter takes place between the years 1640 and 1647. The events are set in the town of Boston in the Massachusetts Bay Colony. Boston was one of the first Puritan settlements in America. The Puritans were known for their rigid morals and stern disapproval of recreation and art. These attitudes were reflected in strict laws that were harshly enforced. Public humiliation was one common form of punishment.

The Puritans in America believed in witchcraft (as did most Europeans at the time). They believed that men and women met with the devil in the wilderness surrounding the settlements. There they signed Satan's book and became wizards and witches who carried out his evil purposes. Satan was referred to as the Black Man in the forest.

Physicians at this time were often called *leeches*. This is because of the practice of using leeches to remove "bad blood" from people who were ill.

Alchemy was a practice somewhere betwee science and magic. Alchemists attempted to tu lead into gold, to create an elixir that wou extend life, and to discover a single cure for diseases.

NATHANIEL HAWTHORNE

The Scarlet Letter

Edited, and with an Introduction,
by Bill Blauvelt

 THE TOWNSEND LIBRARY

THE SCARLET LETTER

TP THE TOWNSEND LIBRARY

For more titles in the Townsend Library,
visit our website: **www.townsendpress.com**

ISBN 13: 978-1-59194-072-2
ISBN 10: 1-59194-072-9

Library of Congress Control Number:
2006926043

Contents

Afterword

Nathaniel Hawthorne completed *The Scarlet Letter* in 1850. He introduces the novel with the following explanation of how he came to write the story:

❧ THE ❧ CUSTOM HOUSE

Introduction to
The Scarlet Letter

For three years—from 1846 to 1849—I worked as a surveyor for the District of Salem, Massachusetts, where I lived. My office was in the Salem Custom House. On the second floor of the Custom House there was a large, unfinished room. The brickwork and bare rafters had never been plastered over and the floor was of rough boards. At one end of this room, with its cobwebs and its coating of dust, there were several barrels piled up. These contained bundles of old and long-forgotten official documents. Some of these documents dated back two hundred years, to the 1640s.

One rainy day when I had nothing better to do, I went into that unfinished room and browsed around in the dusty papers, curious to see if I could learn anything about the history of the early colonial days.

Most of the papers contained dull information about sailing ships that had come to the port—what cargo they had carried, what tariffs they paid, and such. I was about to give up and go downstairs to look for something more interesting to do. But just then I happened to lay my hand on a small package, carefully wrapped up in a piece of ancient yellow parchment. Something about this package aroused my curiosity. I undid the faded red ribbon that tied up the package and discovered that it contained various private documents that were quite different from the dull official records I had been looking through.

But the object in the mysterious package that most drew my attention was a piece of fine red cloth. It was worn and faded. There were traces of gold embroidery that were now dull with age. But in spite of its present condition, even I could see that it had been made with great skill and artistry. As I carefully smoothed out this decaying scarlet rag, it took on the shape of a letter. It was the capital letter A. It was obviously some sort of decoration to be worn on the clothing, but who had worn it and what had it signified? I saw little hope of solving this riddle. And yet it strangely interested me. I could not take my eyes off the once-beautiful object. Whose hand had created it? And for what purpose? I could not begin to guess.

As I pondered the meaning of it, I picked it up and held it against the front of my shirt. It seemed to me—and you will find this hard to believe—it seemed to me, then, that I experienced a strange sensation, not exactly physical, but almost as if I felt a burning heat. It was as if the letter were not made of red cloth but of red-hot iron! I shuddered and let it fall to the floor.

This scarlet letter had so captured my imagination that, up to this moment, I had ignored the small roll of dingy paper that it had been twisted around. I now opened the roll and discovered it contained a reasonably complete explanation of the mysterious red letter.

The letter had been worn by a woman named Hester Prynne. Hester had lived in the Massachusetts colony from 1640 until her death in the late 1690s. In her later years, she had acted as a kind of voluntary nurse for the inhabitants of the area. She apparently had helped those who were ill or in need and she also gave advice, especially in matters of love. Many people thought of her as an angel of mercy, but others found her an intrusive nuisance. The papers also contained some facts about her sufferings in her younger years. Those facts I have put together in the narrative that follows. I have invented some of the details. However, the main facts of the story are just as they appeared in the handwritten document I found in that dusty second floor room.

The more I thought about it, the more fascinated I became with Hester Prynne's story. I was especially haunted by it when I sat alone in my parlor late at night. Illuminated only by the glimmer of the coal-fire and the white light of the moon shining through the window, the objects in the room around me seemed transformed. In this mysterious light, they were no longer the familiar sofa, the table, the bookcase. No, they became invested with a quality of strangeness and remoteness. The light and the stillness of the late hour transformed the usually familiar room into a neutral territory, somewhere between the real world and the world of phantoms, a place where the Actual and the Imaginary may meet. These two worlds—the Actual and the Imaginary— seemed to saturate one another. Each infused the other with its qualities. It became a place where ghosts might enter without frightening us.

It was at such times in my parlor, transformed by the light, by the silence, by the solitude, that I was able to imagine the details that lay behind the facts of Hester Prynne's story.

CHAPTER 1

The Prison Door

A crowd waited in front of the small wooden building. The bearded men were dressed in sad-colored clothing and wore tall gray hats. The women, some wearing hoods, and others bareheaded, wore dresses of somber colors covered by equally drab cloaks.

These Puritans included some of the original founders of the town of Boston. When they had first come here, twelve years earlier, they had arrived in the wilderness of the New World with dreams of creating a perfect society, a Utopia. But their hopes of a perfect place to live were quickly crushed by harsh reality. Shortly after they arrived, it became necessary to set aside one piece of land for a cemetery and another as a site for a prison.

And so, only a dozen years after the settlement of the town, the wooden jail was already marked with weather stains. These and other signs of age gave the dreary building a darkly threatening appearance. The door was massively timbered with oak and studded with iron spikes. The rust on the heavy, dull ironwork looked more ancient than anything else in the New World. In front of the building was a patch of grass, overgrown with straggling weeds. It was as if these ugly weeds had found something agreeable in this soil—the same soil from which sprang that black flower of civilized society, a prison.

But, on one side of the dark and gloomy door, was a wild rosebush. This June day it was covered with delicate red blooms. One could imagine these blossoms offering their fragrance and fragile beauty to the condemned criminal as he came forth from the prison to meet his doom. It was as if the deep heart of Nature could pity him and be kind to him.

CHAPTER 2

The Marketplace

The patch of grass in front of the jail, in Prison Lane, on that June morning in 1642 was filled with solemn men and women. Their eyes were intently fastened on the iron clamped oak door. The sternness of their faces would make one think that they were awaiting the public execution of some hated criminal.

But we cannot draw such a conclusion. The Puritan society of the early Massachusetts Colony was harshly strict and severe. Possibly, a lazy bond-servant or an unruly child was to be taught a lesson at the whipping post. Or maybe a Quaker was to be beaten and chased out of town and into the wilderness for his religious beliefs. Or possibly some poor woman condemned as a witch was to die on the gallows. No matter what the case, the criminal being punished could expect no sympathy from the bystanders, no matter how extreme the punishment.

The women in the crowd outside the prison door seemed particularly interested in the punishment about to take place. One cluster of women was speaking boldly, as the morning sun fell on their broad shoulders and their rosy cheeks.

"Goodwives," said a hard-featured housewife of fifty, "I'll tell you what I think: We women should be put in charge of Hester Prynne's punishment. We are God-fearing church members in good standing. I promise you, that whore wouldn't have gotten off with such a light sentence if she had been judged by the five of us!"

"People say," said another in the group, "that the pastor of her church, the Reverend Arthur Dimmesdale, is grievously saddened that such a scandal as adultery happened in his congregation."

"The magistrates are God-fearing gentlemen, but too merciful, I think," added a third woman, scowling. "At the very least, they should have branded Hester Prynne's forehead with a hot iron. Madam Hester would feel that, I bet! That impudent slut doesn't care what they make her wear on her dress. She can easily hide such a thing and walk through town as boldly as ever!"

A younger woman interrupted this comment. "Yes," she said, speaking softly, "but try as she may to cover the mark, the pain of it will always be in her heart."

"Why waste our time talking of marks and brandings, whether on the breast of her gown or the flesh of her forehead?" cried another woman, the ugliest and the most pitiless of these self-appointed judges. "This woman has brought shame on us all and ought to die. Isn't there a law for it? We know there is, both in the Scripture and in the laws of the colony. Those magistrates who have ignored the law will have only themselves to thank if their own wives and daughters fall into adultery!"

She would have continued, but the rattle of the prison door lock silenced her.

The door of the prison was flung open from within. The grim and grisly figure of the jailer appeared, like a black shadow emerging into the sunshine. He stopped outside the door and reached his right hand back into the darkness of the doorway. He laid his hand on the shoulder of a young woman and drew her forward. As she reached the threshold of the prison door, she shrugged the hand off her shoulder and stepped into the open air, as if by her own free will. Her emergence was marked with natural dignity and force of character. In her arms she held an infant some three months old. The baby blinked and turned its face aside from the bright sunlight.

Until now it had known only the gray twilight of the prison.

The young woman—the mother of the child—stood in plain view of the crowd. Her first impulse was to clasp the infant tightly to her breast, as if to conceal a particular object that was fastened to her dress. Then, realizing that one symbol of her shame would only poorly hide another, she took the baby on her arm. This action revealed, on the breast of her gown, the letter A. It was made of fine red cloth and was surrounded with elaborate embroidery and fantastic flourishes. It had been sewn with a gorgeous luxuriance of artistic imagination and seemed a fitting decoration to the dress she wore. In fact, the letter and her entire dress were of a splendor that went far beyond what was generally allowed by the colony's regulations.

With a burning blush in her cheek but a proud smile on her lips, the young woman surveyed the crowd. She was tall, with dark, flowing hair that gleamed in the sunlight. Her rich complexion highlighted her deep black eyes. Those who had known her before had expected her appearance to be dimmed by a disastrous cloud; but they were astonished to see how her beauty radiated. It was as if that beauty made a halo of the misfortune and dishonor in which she was enveloped. Her dress, which she had created for this occasion while in prison, seemed to express the attitude of her spirit through its wild and picturesque splendor. But it was the Scarlet Letter, embroidered with such extravagance on her dress, that caught the eye of everyone in the crowd. The fanciful symbol of her dishonor seemed to transfigure her with its artistry. It had the effect of a spell, taking her out of the ordinary relations with humanity and enclosing her in a sphere by herself.

"She's quite an artist with her sewing needle, that's for certain," remarked one of the women in the crowd; "but no woman ever contrived such a way of showing off her skill, before this brazen whore came along. How dare she take that symbol of shame and turn it into a thing of pride! Why, she's practically spitting in the faces of our godly magistrates!"

"We should tear that letter from her dress," muttered the eldest of the hags in the group, "and carve the A into her fair flesh! That would be more fitting punishment."

"Hush, my friends!" whispered the youngest woman in the group. "I'll guarantee that every stitch in that letter she has felt in her heart."

The grim jailer now made a gesture with his staff.

"Make way, in the King's name," he cried. "Let us through and, I promise you, Mistress Prynne shall soon stand on the scaffold, where man, woman, and child may all get a good look at her symbol of shame. And a blessing on the righteous Colony of Massachusetts, where evil sin is dragged out into the sunshine! Come along, Madam Hester, and show your scarlet letter in the marketplace!"

The crowd of spectators fell back. Preceded by the jailer, Hester Prynne walked through the crowd toward the place appointed for her punishment. A group of eager and curious schoolboys, understanding only that this event had given them a half-day off from their lessons, ran before her. As they ran, they turned back continually to stare into her face and at the winking baby in her arms and at the shameful letter on her breast.

Although the distance from the prison door to the marketplace was not long, it seemed an unending journey to Hester. In spite of her proud appearance, she felt agony with every footstep, as if her heart had been flung into the street for everyone in the crowd to scorn and trample on. But the crowd would never know what she was feeling to look at her. She appeared to pass calmly through the mass of people and to the platform that stood at the far end of the marketplace, nearly in the shadow of Boston's earliest church.

Hester Prynne ascended the flight of wooden steps to the scaffold. There she stood, at about the height of a man's shoulders above the street, for all to gaze upon.

Had there been a Catholic among the crowd of Puritans, he might have seen in this beautiful woman with the infant in her arms a sight that reminded him of the image of the Blessed Virgin as portrayed in many paintings over the centuries. But unlike that sacred image of sinless motherhood, whose infant was to save the world, here was the stain of deepest sin.

There could be no doubt about the serious nature of her crime and its punishment. The governor, several of his counselors, a judge, and the ministers of the town were assembled on the balcony of the meetinghouse, looking down on the scaffold. And from the ground, the crowd looking up at her was somber and grave. The burden of a thousand unrelenting eyes staring at the symbol of her sin was almost intolerable to Hester. If only they had laughed at her, she could have repaid them with a bitter and scornful smile. But under the leaden weight of solemn silence, she felt as if she must shriek out with the full power of her lungs. She felt herself on the verge of madness.

There were moments when the grim figures around her seemed to become indistinct before her eyes and dissolve into a mass of imperfectly shaped and ghostly images. This Boston street, carved into the edge of the New World wilderness would all but disappear, replaced by figures from other places and other times. Vivid reminiscences of moments from childhood came swarming back upon her—school days, friends, childish quarrels, and little details of daily life as a young girl. Possibly it was instinct that stirred her imagination, to relieve and protect her from the cruel harshness of the reality around her.

Standing at this unhappy spot on the scaffold, she seemed able to look back along the entire path of the life she had traveled since her happy childhood. She saw again her native village, back in England. And there was the gray stone house she had grown up in. It was the house her father had built when he had been a wealthy and respected gentleman from a fine family. But then the family fell on hard times and the grand house took on a decayed, poverty-stricken look. She saw the dear face of her mother, now dead, and the kindly face of her father. She saw her own face, glowing with girlish beauty, reflected in a dusky mirror. And there she gazed upon another face, that of an older man. It was a pale, thin, scholar-like face, with eyes dimmed from many years of poring over ponderous books in lamplight. But those same bleared eyes had a strange, penetrating power when their owner wished to read the human soul. This scholarly figure, Hester recalled, was slightly deformed, with the left shoulder higher than the right.

Next rose in her memory images of the tall, gray houses and narrow streets of Amsterdam, where a new life with the misshapen scholar had awaited her. Finally, this flood of images from the past was replaced by the marketplace of the Puritan settlement, replaced by the townspeople assembled and staring solemnly at her as she stood on the scaffold with an infant in her arms and the letter A, fantastically embroidered with gold thread, on her breast!

Could it be true? She clutched the child so fiercely to her breast that it cried out. She turned her eyes downward at the scarlet letter and touched it with a finger to assure herself that the infant and the shame were real. Yes—these were her realities. All else had vanished!

CHAPTER 3

The Recognition

After a period of time—Hester did not know how long—her attention was diverted from this intense focus on her own realities to the reality of two people at the edge of the crowd surrounding the scaffold. One was an Indian, but the sight of an Indian in the English settlement was not so unusual as to draw her attention. No, it was the white man by the Indian's side who now became the subject of Hester's intense concentration.

This white man was dressed in a strange mixture of European and Native American clothing. He was small. The features of his thin face suggested a remarkable intelligence. It was as if he had so cultivated his mental part that the effort had molded his physical appearance to match. It was evident to Hester that one of this man's shoulders rose higher than the other. At the first instant that she perceived the face and the slight deformity of the body, she clutched the infant in her arms with such force that the baby uttered a cry of pain. But the mother did not seem to hear it.

The stranger had arrived in the marketplace some time before she saw him. His first glance at Hester had been careless; it was like that of a man used to looking inward, a man to whom outward matters were of little importance. Quickly, however, his look had become sharp and penetrating. A writhing horror twisted itself across his features, like a snake gliding swiftly over them. His face darkened with some powerful emotion. Then, through an effort of will, he regained a look of calmness. The dark emotion sank into the depths of his nature. When he realized that the eyes of Hester were fastened on his own, he saw that she appeared to recognize him. He calmly put his finger across his lips, in a sign that she should not reveal that she recognized him.

A moment later, he turned to a townsman standing near him and asked courteously, "Good Sir, who is this woman? And why is she facing this public shame?"

"You must be a stranger to Boston, friend," answered the townsman. "Otherwise, you would have heard of Hester Prynne and her evil doings. She has caused a great scandal in godly Reverend Dimmesdale's church."

"You are right, I am a stranger," replied the misshapen man. "I have had terrible luck on sea and on land and have long been held captive by the Indians to the south of here. I have been led here by this Indian to be bought out of my captivity by the authorities of Boston. But tell me, what are Hester Prynne's—do I have her name right?—what are this woman's offenses that have brought her to such punishment?"

"Well, friend, you sound as if you have had a long and troubled journey," the townsman said. "After so much time in the wilderness, I think it must warm your heart to be back in a land where evil is searched out and punished in full view of the people. That woman was the wife of a learned Englishman. They had moved to Amsterdam for a time. Then he decided to try his luck here in Massachusetts. He sent his wife on ahead, while he wrapped up his affairs in Amsterdam. Hester Prynne has lived here in Boston for two years with no word from her husband. And you can see what has resulted from this young woman being left here on her own."

"I understand your meaning," the stranger said with a bitter smile. "The learned husband should have learned this from his books. And who, sir, is the father of the baby?"

"That, my friend, remains a great mystery," replied the townsman. "Hester Prynne refuses to answer that question. The guilty father may be standing in this very crowd, forgetting that God sees him."

"Perhaps the learned husband should come himself to look into this mystery," observed the stranger, with another smile.

"It would be good for him to do so, if he is still alive," responded the townsman. "She could have received the death penalty for her sin. But our judges believed that one so young and fair as she is must have been tempted into her sin by the man. They also recognized that her husband may be at the bottom of the sea. Therefore, they showed great mercy; they sentenced her to stand three hours on the platform and then, when she is released from the prison, to wear a mark of shame on her dress for the rest of her life."

"A wise sentence, indeed," remarked the stranger. "She will act as a living sermon against sin for as long as she lives. It is unfortunate, however, that her partner in this evil does not stand on the scaffold beside her. But he will be known!—he will be known!"

During this time, Hester Prynne had been gazing at the stranger from her place on the platform. Her stare had been so intense that all other objects in the visible world seemed to vanish, leaving only him and her. She could not help but feel that it was better to see him in this setting than to meet him face to face, the two of them alone together.

She was aroused from these thoughts by a loud and solemn voice behind and above her: "Hester Prynne!"

The voice was that of John Wilson, the oldest and most revered minister in Boston. As Hester turned and looked up at the balcony, she saw the imposing figure of Governor Bellingham. He was surrounded by the other distinguished rulers of the community. They were good and wise elders. But it would have been difficult to find a group of men less capable of sitting in judgment on an erring woman's heart. These solemn men were not equipped to disentangle this mesh of good and evil. Hester grew pale and trembled as she looked up toward these ponderous men.

"Hester Prynne!" repeated the Reverend Mr. Wilson. His gray eyes were used to the dimmed light of his study; they twinkled in the unadulterated sunshine. He looked like a dim portrait found at the beginning of a thick book of ancient sermons; and he had no more right than one of those portraits would have, to step forth, as he did now, and meddle with a question of human guilt, passion, and anguish.

"Hester Prynne," Wilson said, "I have struggled to convince Mr. Dimmesdale to confront you here in public about the vileness and blackness of your sin." Here he paused and laid his hand on the shoulder of a pale young man beside him. "As your minister, he knows your temperament better than I. He would better know how to overcome your refusal to reveal the name of the man who tempted you into this sin. But he has disagreed with me. He has said it wrongs the very nature of a woman to lay open her heart's secrets in such broad daylight. I have tried to convince him that the sin lay in the commission of the sin, not in the public revelation of it. What do you say, brother Dimmesdale? Will it be you or me that deals with this poor sinner's soul?"

There was a moment of silence. Then Governor Bellingham spoke. "Good Master Dimmesdale, the responsibility of this woman's soul lies primarily with you. It is only proper that you urge this woman to repent and, to prove her repentance, to confess who the father is."

With this, the eyes of the whole crowd turned upon the Reverend Mr. Dimmesdale. He was a handsome man with large, brown, melancholy eyes. His mouth suggested a vast power of self-restraint. This young clergyman was already well respected in the community. Having arrived from one of the great English universities, he had brought his vast learning to this wild forest land. But in spite of his scholarly achievements, there was an air about him of one who felt at odds with the rest of human society. This revealed itself in an apprehensive, a startled, a half-frightened look that suggested a simple and almost childlike quality. It was, perhaps, this last quality that gave his public statements a freshness and dewy purity of thought. Many said that when he spoke it affected them like the speech of an angel.

This, then, was the young man whom the Reverend Mr. Wilson and the governor had called upon to speak to Hester. The trying nature of his position drove the blood from him cheek and made his lips tremble.

"Speak to the woman, my brother," said Mr. Wilson. "It is of the utmost importance to her soul—and to yours as she is one of your parishioners. Urge her to confess the truth and tell us the name of the man who has led her into sin."

The Reverend Mr. Dimmesdale bent his head, seemingly in silent prayer, and then came forward.

"Hester Prynne," he said, leaning over the balcony and looking down directly into her eyes, "you have heard what the good Mr. Wilson has said. And you see how important a matter this is to me. For the sake of your soul, I urge you to speak out the name of your fellow sinner and fellow sufferer. It is a mistake to be silent out of pity and tenderness for him. Believe me, Hester, if he were to step down from a high place and stand beside you on your pedestal of shame, it would be better for him than to hide a guilty heart throughout his life. Your silence will only tempt and compel him to add hypocrisy to sin. Heaven has granted you the opportunity to work out an open triumph over evil within yourself. Do not deny him the same chance, for perhaps he does not have the courage to grasp the opportunity himself."

The young pastor's voice was tremblingly sweet, rich, deep, and broken. The feeling that it shed upon the listeners caused it to vibrate within all hearts. Even the poor baby in Hester's arms was affected. The infant directed its gaze toward Mr. Dimmesdale and held up its little arms with a half-pleased, half-sorrowful murmur. So powerful seemed the minister's words that the people could not believe that Hester Prynne would not speak the man's name—or that the guilty one would not voluntarily step forth and join Hester on the scaffold.

Hester shook her head.

"Woman, do not overstep the limits of Heaven's mercy!" cried the Reverend Mr. Wilson, more harshly than before. "Speak out the name! That, and your repentance, may be sufficient to remove the scarlet letter from your breast."

"Never!" replied Hester Prynne, looking not at Mr. Wilson, but into the deep and troubled eyes of the younger clergyman. "The letter is too deeply branded into my heart. You cannot take it off. And I wish that I could suffer his agony as well as my own!"

"Speak, woman!" said another voice, coldly and sternly, proceeding from the crowd about the scaffold. "Speak, and give your child a father!"

"I will not speak!" answered Hester, turning pale as death, but responding to this voice, which she too surely recognized. "And my child must seek a heavenly Father. She shall never know an earthly one!"

"She will not speak!" murmured Mr. Dimmesdale, leaning over the balcony with his hand upon his heart. He drew back, taking a deep breath. "Wondrous strength and generosity of a woman's heart! She will not speak!"

The Reverend Wilson was prepared for Hester's stubborn refusal. He launched into a sermon on the horrors of sin. He spoke for more than an hour, making frequent references to the letter on Hester's dress. So forcefully did he dwell on that symbol that it assumed new terrors in the imaginations of the people; it seemed to derive its scarlet color from the very fires of Hell.

Hester Prynne, meanwhile, kept her place on the pedestal of shame, with glazed eyes and an air of weary indifference. She had withstood that morning all that nature could endure. She now retreated into stony insensibility while the voice of the preacher thundered on.

The infant pierced the air with its screams. Hester mechanically tried to hush it, but she seemed hardly to sympathize with its troubles.

When Hester's three hours on the scaffold were up, she was taken back to prison with the same insensible appearance. The heavy oaken door studded with iron spikes swung open and she was led inside, vanishing from the public gaze into the darkness. It was whispered, by those who peered after her, that the scarlet letter threw a lurid gleam along the dark passageway of the interior.

CHAPTER 4

The Interview

After her return to the prison, Hester Prynne was in a state of extreme nervous excitement. Master Brackett, the jailer, felt it necessary to watch her constantly to be sure she did not harm herself or the infant. As night approached, it was impossible to calm her wild disobedience with scoldings or threats of punishment. By this time, the baby seemed also to have absorbed all the turmoil, anguish, and despair that pervaded the mother's system; it writhed with convulsions of pain. Master Brackett determined that a doctor was needed. He brought a physician to Hester's cell. He described this doctor as a man of skill in all Christian modes of physical science. The man was also, Master Brackett reported, knowledgeable in the medicinal herbs and roots that grew in the forest.

Behind Master Brackett in the doorway of Hester's dismal cell stood the misshapen stranger who had been so interested in learning about Hester as she stood on the scaffold that morning. He had been given a bed in the prison not as punishment, but because he needed a place to stay until the magistrates had met with the Indian sagamores to discuss his ransom. The jailer announced that the man's name was Roger Chillingworth. When Hester Prynne saw him, she immediately became as still as death, although the child continued to moan.

"Please, my friend, leave me alone with my patient," said the physician. "Trust me, good jailer, you shall soon have quiet here."

"If you can accomplish that," answered Master Brackett, "I shall think you a man of skill indeed! The woman has been like someone possessed. I am ready to take a whip to her to drive Satan out of her."

After the jailer left, Roger Chillingworth looked at Hester in silence for a moment. Then he turned his attention to the crying infant who lay writhing on the trundle bed. He examined her carefully and then opened a leather case. It appeared to contain certain medical preparations, one of which he mixed with a cup of water.

"My old studies in alchemy," he said, "along with the knowledge I gained during my past year among the savages in the wilderness have made me a better physician than most who have a medical degree. Here, woman! This child is yours— she is none of mine—and she will not recognize my voice or my face. Give her this medicine, therefore, with your own hand."

Hester pushed away the offered medicine, looking at him fearfully. "Would you avenge yourself on an innocent babe?" she whispered.

"Foolish woman!" responded the physician, half-coldly, half-soothingly. "Do you think I would harm this misbegotten and miserable child? The medicine is good. Were it my own child—my own, as well as yours—I could do no better for it."

Still she hesitated, so he took the infant in his arms and gave it the medicine himself. Soon the child's moans subsided and its convulsive tossings ceased.

The physician next turned his attention to the mother. He calmly felt her pulse and looked into her eyes. His gaze made her heart shrink and shudder—it was so familiar, yet so strange and cold. When the doctor had determined her condition, he mixed another medicine with water.

"I have learned many new secrets in the wilderness," Chillingworth remarked, "and here is one of them. It is a recipe that an Indian taught me. It may be less soothing than a sinless conscience. That I cannot give you. But it will calm you."

He held the cup out to Hester. She took the cup from his hand with a slow, earnest look into his face. It was not precisely a look of fear, but it was full of doubt and questioning as to what his purposes might be.

"I have thought of death," she said. "I have even wished for it. But if death be in this cup, I urge you to think again, before I drink it."

"Drink, then," he replied, still with the same cold composure. "Do you know me so little, Hester? Even if I dream of a scheme of vengeance, what better way than to let you live so that this burning shame will blaze on your breast?"

As he spoke, he touched the scarlet letter with his index finger. As he did so, it seemed to Hester that the letter scorched into her breast, as if it were red-hot.

"Live, therefore," he continued with a smile, "and carry your doom with you before the eyes of men and women—before the eyes of your child! Now drink."

Without further delay, Hester Prynne drained the cup. The physician motioned for her to sit on the bed, next to the sleeping child. As she did so, he drew up the stool and sat facing her.

"Hester," he said, "I do not ask why or how this has happened. The reason is obvious. It was my foolishness and your weakness. I—a book-worm in great libraries, a man already in decay, having given my best years to feed the hungry dream of knowledge—what had I to do with youth and beauty such as yours! Misshapen from the hour of my birth, how could I delude myself with the idea that intellectual gifts might hide physical deformity from a young girl's eyes! If I were truly wise, I might have foreseen this—foreseen that, when I came out of the vast and dismal forest and into this settlement of Christian men, the very first object to meet my eyes would be you, Hester, standing in shame for all to see. Were I truly wise, I might have seen, when we came down the church steps together, a married pair, that this scarlet letter blazed at the end of our path!"

"You know," Hester said, "that I was frank with you. I felt no love for you, nor did I pretend to."

"True," he replied. "It was my foolishness. But up until then, my life had been so cheerless! My heart was lonely and chill and without a household fire. I longed to kindle one. It didn't seem such a wild dream that—old and misshapen as I was—the simple happiness of human companionship might yet be mine. I drew you into my heart. Your presence created warmth there. And I tried to win you with that warmth you created."

"I have greatly wronged you," murmured Hester.

"We   have   wronged   each   other," he

answered. "Mine was the first wrong, when I betrayed your youth into a false and unnatural relation with my decay. Therefore, I seek no vengeance and I plot no evil against you. Between us, the scale hangs fairly balanced. But, Hester, the man lives who has wronged us both. Who is he?"

"Do not ask me that!" replied Hester, looking firmly into his face. "You will never know!"

"Never, you say?" he said, with a smile of dark and self-relying intelligence. "Never know him! Believe me, Hester, in the real outward world and in the invisible world of thought, there are few things hidden from the man who earnestly devotes himself to the solution of a mystery. You may conceal him from the magistrates and ministers. But I search with other senses than they possess. I shall seek this man as I have sought truth in books, as I have sought gold in alchemy. I shall see him tremble. At that same moment, I shall feel myself shudder, suddenly and unexpectedly. Sooner or later, he will be mine!"

The eyes of the wrinkled scholar glowed so intensely upon her that Hester clasped her hands over her heart, dreading that he would read the secret there.

"He wears no letter of shame, as you do," he went on, with a look of confidence. "But I shall read it in his heart. Yet, do not fear for him. I will not take his life. Nor will I harm his reputation if he is, as I suspect, a respected man. Let him live! Let him hide himself in outward honor. Nevertheless, he shall be mine!"

"Your actions are merciful," said Hester, bewildered and appalled. "But your words reveal a demon."

"One thing, my dear wife, I must insist upon," continued the scholar. "You have kept the secret of your lover. Likewise, you must keep my secret. No one here knows who I am. Breathe not to any human soul that you did ever call me husband. I shall stay here. Here I find a woman, a man, and a child with whom I have a close bond. No matter whether love or hate, right or wrong—it is a human bond. My home is where the three of you are, Hester Prynne. But betray me not!"

"Why are you doing this?" asked Hester, shrinking from this agreement. "Why not publicly say who you are and cast me off at once?"

"It may be," he replied, "because I do not wish the dishonor that besmirches the husband of a faithless woman. It may be for other reasons. But it is my purpose to live and die unknown. That is why I have taken the name Roger Chillingworth. Therefore, let your husband be as one who is already dead and of whom no news will ever come. Acknowledge me not by word, by sign, by look. Above all, breathe not this secret to your lover. If you fail me in this, beware! His fame, his position, his life will be in my hands. Beware!"

"I will keep your secret as I have kept his," said Hester.

"Swear it!" he demanded.

"I give my word."

"And now, Mistress Prynne," said old Roger Chillingworth, "I leave you alone with your infant and your letter. How is it, Hester? Must you wear the letter in your sleep? Are you not afraid of nightmares and hideous dreams?"

"Why do you smile at me that way," asked Hester, troubled at the expression in his eyes. "Are you like the Devil that haunts the forest? Have you enticed me into an oath that will prove the ruin of my soul?"

"Not your soul," he answered, with another smile. "No, not yours!"

CHAPTER 5

Hester at Her Needle

The day on which Hester Prynne's prison term came to an end, the massive oaken door studded with iron spikes was thrown open and she emerged into the sunshine. It felt to her as if the sun's only purpose was to reveal the scarlet letter on her breast. Her first footsteps into the open signaled the beginning of a much greater torment than she had suffered that day, three months before, when she had walked to the scaffold. That had been a single event and she had been able to summon her strength and convert the scene into a kind of lurid triumph. But now, with this unattended walk from her prison door, began the pain of daily life. Tomorrow would bring its own trial; so would the next day, and so would the next. Each day would bring its own trial, the same trial she suffered under now as she walked forth alone. If she did not find the strength in the resources of her own nature to carry forward in daily life, she would sink beneath it. The accumulating days and years would pile up their misery on the heap of shame. She would give up her individuality and become the general symbol of sin that the preacher would point to. Daughters would be taught to look at her, with the scarlet letter flaming on her breast, as the figure, the body, the reality of sin. And even over her grave, the shameful letter would be her only monument.

It may seem odd that this woman would continue to call this place home. She was free to return to Europe, where she could hide her identity in a new life. And the paths of the dark forest were also open to her; there the wildness of her nature might find shelter among the inhabitants of that untamed world. But there is a sensation, a force irresistible and inevitable, that almost invariably compels human beings to linger around and haunt, ghostlike, the spot where some great event has given color to and saddened their lifetime. Her sin had become the roots she had struck into the New England soil. It was as if a new birth had converted the wilderness of this forest land into Hester Prynne's wild and dreary, but lifelong home. All other places on earth— even the village in England where she had spent her happy youth—were foreign to her, in comparison. The chain that bound her here was of iron links that could never be broken.

It might be, too, that another feeling kept her in this grim community. Here walked the feet of one with whom she felt herself connected in a union. And that union, unrecognized on earth, might bring them together at the final judgment. When this thought entered her mind, she seized it with a passionate and desperate joy, only to cast it aside a moment later. Whenever this thought struggled out of her heart like a serpent from its hole, she attempted to drive it out. Most of the time, she was able to convince herself that, since this had been the scene of her guilt, it should also be the scene of her earthly punishment. In that way, she might eventually purge her soul and achieve a new sort of purity.

Hester Prynne, therefore, did not flee. On the outskirts of town there was a small thatched cottage. It lay at the very edge of the peninsula, not close to any other houses. It had been built by an early settler but then abandoned because it was too isolated from the society of town. It stood on the shore, looking west toward the forest-covered hills across a basin of the sea. The magistrates, who still kept watch over Hester, granted her permission to establish herself in the little, lonesome dwelling. A mystic shadow of suspicion immediately attached itself to the spot.

Young children would creep close to the cottage to see Hester sewing at the cottage window, or standing in the doorway or working in her garden or coming along the path to town; then, seeing the scarlet letter on her breast, these children would scamper off with a strange, contagious fear.

Hester was without a friend on earth who dared to show himself. But, lonely as her situation was, she was well able to provide for herself and her child. Her skill at needlework insured that the two of them would never want for food. In general, the Puritan dress was quite plain. The officials who oversaw public ceremonies, however, required magnificent though somber clothing—gorgeously embroidered gloves, elegant deep ruffs. Funerals, too, required finely decorated clothing, whether for the dead body or the grieving survivors. And beautifully decorated baby linen was also in demand.

By degrees her handiwork became the fashion. Hester had enough work to keep her needle busy for as many hours as she wished to make use of it. The needlework of her sinful hands was seen on the ruff of the governor; military men wore it on their scarves, and the ministers on their ceremonial robes; it decked the little baby's cap; it was shut up, to be mildewed and molder away, in the coffins of the dead. But not once was she called to use her skill to embroider the white veil that was to cover the pure blushes of a bride. The exception showed the relentlessness with which society frowned upon her sin.

Hester could have earned enough to live very well from her needlework, but she chose not to. Her own dress was made of coarse material and a somber color—except for the scarlet letter that adorned it. Her child's clothing, on the other hand, was one place where she allowed her fanciful imagination to come into play. Except for the small amount spent to decorate the child's clothing, Hester put all of her extra earnings into charity. She spent much of her time making coarse garments for the poor.

Hester's charitable work was the only way that she could feel a connection with the society around her. In every other way, she was as alone as if she inhabited another sphere. Society had banished her. In spite of all of her interaction with others around her needlework, there was nothing that made her feel as if she belonged to the community. Everyone she came in contact with—including the poor she did so much for— scorned and insulted her, either openly or with subtle looks. Hester never responded to these attacks, except by a flush of crimson rising over her pale cheek. She was patient—almost a martyr.

The punishment that the magistrates had contrived for her was never-ending. If she entered a church, she often found herself to be the subject of the sermon. Even on the street, clergymen would point her out as a lesson to others. She grew to dread children. Their parents had taught them that there was something horrible in this dreary woman who glided silently through town, her only companion her own child. Children would run after her at a distance with shrill cries, calling her names they did not understand. Another torture was when strangers came to town and gazed on the letter for the first time. Their look branded the scarlet letter afresh into her soul. Hester always suffered dreadful agony when she felt a human eye on the symbol.

But occasionally—perhaps once in many months—she felt an eye gazing at the letter that seemed to give momentary relief. It felt for that moment as if her agony were shared. The next instant, back it all rushed again, with still a deeper throb of pain; for, in that brief interval, she had sinned anew. Had Hester sinned alone?

Hester's imagination was somewhat affected by the strange and solitary anguish of her life. From time to time it seemed to her that she possessed a new sense, a new awareness of others. Was it possible that, if truth were shown everywhere, a scarlet letter would blaze forth on the breast of others besides herself? She could not dare to let herself consider this idea. Sometimes the red symbol of shame on her breast would give a sympathetic throb. "What evil thing is at hand?" she would say to herself. Then, looking around, she would discover that the only other human being in sight was some honored minister or magistrate. At other times, the letter would seem to give off an energy, as if to say, "Look, Hester, here is a companion." Looking up, she would see the eyes of a young maiden glancing at the scarlet letter shyly, with a faint, chill crimson on her cheeks.

There was a rumor among some of the townspeople that the letter was not merely scarlet cloth but that it was red-hot with infernal fire and that it could be seen glowing whenever Hester walked about at night. And it must be said that it seared Hester's breast so deeply that perhaps there was more truth to this rumor than our modern habit of skepticism might wish to admit.

CHAPTER 6

Pearl

Hester watched her infant become every day more beautiful. The child had an intelligence about her that threw its sunshine over its tiny features. The child was Hester's Pearl—for so she had named her. The child, however, had none of the calm, white, unimpassioned luster that the name would suggest. Rather, Hester had named the infant Pearl as being of great price—purchased with all she had. How odd it seemed that human justice had marked this woman's sin by a scarlet letter that isolated her from all human sympathy. God, on the other hand, had given Hester this lovely child, as a direct consequence of her sin. But she knew her sin had been evil; she could have no faith, therefore, that its result would be for good. Day after day, she looked fearfully into the child's expanding nature. She dreaded that would detect some dark and wild peculiarity that reflected the guiltiness that had brought Pearl into existence.

Certainly, there was no physical defect in the child. She could have been born into Eden as a plaything for the angels. To complement the child's natural perfection, Hester had purchased the finest materials available for her clothing. She had then given her imagination full play when creating dresses for little Pearl to wear in public. This combination of physical perfection and magnificent clothing created an absolute circle of radiance around the child. In this one child there were many children, ranging from the wild-flower prettiness of a peasant baby to the elegance of an infant princess. And through all of this glimmered Pearl's trait of passion.

But for all of her range of qualities, Pearl seemed unable to adapt to the world into which she was born. She could not be made to obey rules. Hester could only account for the child's character by recalling her own temperament while she had carried the child within her. Hester's spirit had been at warfare during those months. Now, Hester could see in Pearl her own wild, desperate, defiant mood.

At first, Hester tried to impose a tender, but strict control over the child. But the task was beyond her skill. Ultimately, she was compelled to stand aside and permit the child to be swayed by her own impulses. Hester quickly came to know a certain peculiar look that came over Pearl. The look—so intelligent, yet so perverse, sometimes so malicious—caused Hester to question at these moments whether Pearl was a human child. Whenever that look appeared in her, it was as if she were a spirit, hovering in the air, ready to vanish at an instant. Hester would rush toward the little elf and take her in her arms, as if to assure herself that the child really was flesh and blood. But Pearl's laughter when she was caught, though full of merriment and music, made her mother more doubtful than before.

At such moments, Hester sometimes burst into passionate tears. There was no way to foresee how Pearl would react to this. Sometimes she would clench her little fists and harden her little features into a stern look of discontent. Other times, she would laugh anew, like a thing incapable of and unaware of human sorrow. Or—occasionally—she would be convulsed with a rage of grief. But these moods would pass as suddenly as they came. Hester's only real comfort was when the child lay peacefully sleeping. Then Hester was sure of her and tasted hours of quiet, sad, delicious happiness. This would last until little Pearl awoke—perhaps with that perverse expression glimmering from beneath her opening eyelids.

Pearl was soon old enough to play with other children. What happiness would it have been, could Hester have heard her clear, bird-like voice mingled with the roar of other childish voices. But this could never be. Pearl was a born outcast. An imp of evil, emblem and product of sin, she had no right among christened infants. Pearl seemed to comprehend that destiny had drawn a circle round about her that cut her off from the rest of society.

In all of Hester's walks about town, Pearl appeared beside her. They would see the children of the settlement playing their Puritan games. Pearl gazed intently at these children, but never tried to join them. If the children gathered about her, as they sometimes did, Pearl would snatch up stones to fling at them and make shrill, incoherent exclamations that had the sound of a witch's curse in some unknown tongue.

The truth was that the little Puritans, intolerant as they were, had got a vague idea of something unearthly and horrible in the mother and child. In their hearts, the children scorned these two, and with their tongues, they frequently abused both mother and child with their insults. Mother and daughter stood together in the same circle of seclusion from human society.

At home, within and around her mother's cottage, Pearl created all the companions she needed. The spell of life went forth from her ever-creative spirit. She could make a stick, a bunch of rags, a flower become the puppets of her witchcraft. She would adapt them to whatever drama occupied the stage of her inner world at the time. For Pearl, the pine trees, aged, black, and solemn, and flinging melancholy groans on the breeze, needed little transformation to become her Puritan elders. The ugliest weeds in the garden were their children, who Pearl would knock down and uproot most unmercifully. In her imaginative energy, Pearl was like other children. But the hostility she showed toward her inventions set her apart. She never created a friend but always armed enemies against whom she rushed to battle.

Gazing at Pearl, Hester Prynne often dropped her needlework to her lap and cried out in agony, "O Father in Heaven—if Thou are still my Father—what is the being which I have brought into the world?" And Pearl, overhearing, would turn her beautiful little face upon her mother, smile with sprite-like intelligence, and resume her play.

As an infant, the very first thing which Pearl had noticed was not, as with other babies, her mother's smile. The first object of which she seemed to become aware was the scarlet letter on Hester's breast. One day, as her mother stooped over the cradle, the infant's eyes had been caught by the glimmering gold embroidery about the letter. Putting her little hand up, she grasped at it, smiling. Gasping for breath, Hester instinctively pulled back. In response, little Pearl looked into her mother's eyes and smiled. From that moment forward, Hester never felt a moment's safety, except when the child was asleep. It is true that weeks would sometimes pass during which Pearl's gaze might never once be fixed on the scarlet letter. But then, again, it would come, like a stroke of sudden death, and always with that peculiar smile and odd expression of the eyes.

Once, a freakish, elfish look had come into the child's eyes. Hester had been looking at her own image reflected in the small black mirror of Pearl's eye. But what she saw was not her own image, but another face, like a miniature portrait. It was a face, fiend-like, full of smiling malice. It was as if an evil spirit possessed the child and had just then peeped forth in mockery. And many times after that, Hester had been tortured with that same illusion.

One summer afternoon after Pearl grew big enough to run about, she amused herself by gathering handfuls of wildflowers and flinging them, one by one, at her mother's breast. Whenever she hit the scarlet letter, she danced up and down like a little elf. Hester's impulse was to cover the letter with her hand, but instead she sat, pale as death, looking sadly into little Pearl's wild eyes. Every flower that hit the letter felt like a wound to Hester. At last, Pearl tired of the game. The child stood still and gazed at Hester, with that little, laughing image of a fiend peeping out—or, whether it peeped or not, so Hester imagined it—from the unfathomable abyss of her black eyes.

"Child, what are you?" cried the mother.

"I am your little Pearl!" answered the child. But, while she said it, Pearl laughed and began to dance up and down, with the gestures of a little imp.

"Are you my child, in truth?" asked Hester.

"Yes, I am little Pearl!" repeated the child, continuing her antics.

"You are not my child! You are no Pearl of mine!" said the mother, half-playfully, in spite of her deep suffering. "Tell me, then, what you are, and who sent you here."

"Tell me, Mother!" said the child seriously, coming up to Hester and pressing herself close to her knees. "Do tell me."

"Your Heavenly Father sent you!" answered Hester Prynne.

But she said it with a hesitation that did not escape the child. Whether moved only by her ordinary impishness or because an evil spirit prompted her, she put up her small forefinger and touched the scarlet letter.

"He did not send me!" she cried positively. "I have no Heavenly Father!"

"Hush, Pearl, hush! You must not talk so!" answered the mother, suppressing a groan. "He sent us all into the world. He sent even me. And he sent you as well. If you don't think so, strange and elfish child, then where did you come from?"

"Tell me! Tell me!" repeated Pearl, no longer seriously, but laughing and dancing about. "It is you that must tell me!"

But Hester did not answer, for she was lost in a maze of doubt. She remembered the talk of some of the townspeople. After they had witnessed Pearl's behavior, they had hinted that poor little Pearl was a demon offspring, sent to promote some foul and wicked purpose.

CHAPTER 7

The Governor's Hall

Hester Prynne went, one day, to the mansion of Governor Bellingham. She was delivering a pair of gloves, which she had embroidered to his order. He needed them for some great occasion of state.

But another and far more important reason moved Hester to seek an interview at this time with such a powerful official. She had heard that there was a plan devised by some of the leading inhabitants of the community to take her child from her. These people argued that, if Pearl was of demon origin, Hester would have a much better chance of redeeming her soul without the child. On the other hand, if Pearl was not in fact a demon, the child would receive a much better moral education under the guardianship of someone other than Hester.

Full of concern, Hester set forth from her solitary cottage. Little Pearl, of course, was her companion. She was now old enough to run lightly along by her mother's side and was constantly in motion. Pearl's rich and luxuriant beauty glowed forth in her intense eyes and her deep, glossy brown hair. There was fire throughout her; she seemed the unpremeditated offshoot of a passionate moment. She was dressed in a crimson velvet tunic embroidered with fantasies and flourishes of gold thread. Dashing along the path, she seemed the very brightest little jet of flame that ever danced upon the earth.

A remarkable quality of Pearl's dress, and of her whole appearance, was that it inevitably reminded one of the letter Hester wore. It was the scarlet letter in another form, the scarlet letter endowed with life!

As Hester and her mother reached the edge of town, a group of Puritan children looked up from their somber play.

"There is the woman with the scarlet letter and her wicked child," they said amongst themselves. "Let's throw mud at them!"

But Pearl frowned and made threatening gestures. Then she made a sudden rush at the knot of her enemies and sent them running. She resembled a pestilence—some scarlet fever—whose mission it was to punish the sins of the rising generation. The victory accomplished, Pearl returned quietly to her mother and looked up smiling into her face.

Without further adventure, they reached the

mansion of Governor Bellingham. There was a freshness to this large house, a cheerfulness gleaming forth from the sunny windows. The walls were overspread with a kind of stucco in which fragments of broken glass were plentifully intermixed. As a result, when the sunshine fell slanting over the front of the house, it glittered and sparkled as if diamonds had been flung against it by the double handful. The brilliancy might have been more fitting for Aladdin's palace than it was for the mansion of a grave old Puritan ruler. It was further decorated with strange, mysterious designs, which had been drawn into the stucco when it was first laid on.

Pearl, looking at this bright wonder of a house, began to caper and dance. She demanded that the whole expanse of sunshine be stripped off the front and given to her to play with.

"No, my little Pearl!" said her mother. "You must gather your own sunshine. I have none to give you."

They approached the door. Lifting the iron doorknocker, Hester Prynne rapped firmly. Her summons was answered by a servant.

"Is the worshipful Governor Bellingham in?" Hester asked.

"Yes, he is here," replied the young man. "But he is speaking with three men at the moment and cannot be disturbed."

"Then I will wait," Hester announced, stepping through the doorway.

"Very well," replied the servant, and he left them alone in the entrance hall.

The hall ran the entire depth of the house, with all the other rooms opening off of it. At the far end was a large bright bow window that reached to the floor and gave access to the garden. The furniture of the hall consisted of some ponderous chairs, the backs of which were elaborately carved with wreaths of oaken flowers. A similarly decorated massive oaken table sat in the middle of the space.

On the wall hung a row of portraits of the governor's ancestors. Some were wearing armor; others were dressed in robes of peace. All gazed sternly down as if they were ghosts, intolerant and critical of the living guests in the hall.

About halfway down the oaken panels that lined the hall hung a suit of armor. The helmet and breastplate were so highly polished that they glowed with white radiance and scattered illumination about the room.

Little Pearl—who was greatly pleased with the gleaming armor as she had been with the glittering front of the house—spent some time looking into the polished mirror of the breastplate.

"Mother," she cried, "I see you here. Look! Look!"

To humor the child, Hester looked. She saw that, as a result of the distorting effect of the convex mirror, the scarlet letter was represented in exaggerated and gigantic proportions. It was the most prominent feature of her appearance. In truth, she seemed absolutely hidden behind it. Pearl pointed upward, also, at a similar reflection in the helmet. The child smiled with her look of elfish intelligence. That look of naughty merriment was similarly reflected in the mirror. It, like the letter, was so exaggerated that Hester felt she could not be looking at the image of her own child but rather at the image of an imp who was seeking to mold itself into Pearl's shape.

"Come along, Pearl," she said, drawing the child away. "Come and look into this pretty garden."

Pearl ran to the bow window at the further end of the hall and looked out along the vista of garden-walk, carpeted with closely shaven grass and bordered with some shrubbery. Unlike the decorative English gardens, however, this New England garden had cabbages and pumpkin vines growing in plain sight. There were, however, a few rose bushes and a number of apple trees.

Pearl, seeing the rose bushes, began to cry for a red rose and would not be pacified.

"Hush, child, hush!" said her mother earnestly. "Do not cry, dear little Pearl! I hear voices in the garden. The governor is coming and other gentlemen along with him."

Pearl, in utter scorn of her mother's attempt to quiet her, gave an unearthly scream and then became silent.

CHAPTER 8

The Elf-Child
and the Minister

Governor Bellingham appeared to be showing off his estate to his three guests. Next to the governor walked the worthy Reverend John Wilson. Wilson suggested that pears and peaches might be grown in the garden. The reverend had a taste for all good and comfortable things, in spite of the sternness of his warnings about such worldly matters in his sermons.

Behind the governor and Mr. Wilson walked the Reverend Arthur Dimmesdale and old Roger Chillingworth. Chillingworth had been settled in the town for two or three years. In that time he had become a friend and physician to the young Mr. Dimmesdale, whose health had severely suffered lately as a result of his self-sacrifice to his pastoral duties.

The governor ascended the two steps leading to the bow window. Throwing open the windows he found himself close to little Pearl, who stood just inside, looking out at him. The shadow of the curtain fell on Hester Prynne and partially concealed her.

"What have we here?" said Governor Bellingham, looking with surprise at the scarlet little figure before him. "How did such a guest get into my hall?"

"Indeed!" cried good old Mr. Wilson. "What little bird of scarlet plumage is this? Are you a Christian child, eh? Or are you one of those naughty elfs or fairies that we thought we left behind in merry old England?"

"I am mother's child," answered the scarlet vision, "and my name is Pearl."

"Pearl?—Ruby, rather!—or Coral!—or Red Rose, at the very least, judging by the color of your dress," the old minister answered, putting his hand out in a vain attempt to pat little Pearl on the cheek. But where is your mother? Ah, I see her there in the shadow," he added. Then, turning to Governor Bellingham, he whispered, "This is the very child we were talking about— and her mother, Hester Prynne."

"Is that so?" said the governor. "She comes at a good time. We will look into this matter immediately."

Governor Bellingham stepped through the window into the hall, followed by his three guests.

"Hester Prynne," he said, fixing his naturally stern gaze on her, "there has been a serious question concerning you lately. We have discussed at length whether we can, in good conscience, trust the immortal soul of this child to the guidance of one who has stumbled and fallen morally. Do you not think it better for the child's moral welfare that she be taken from you so that she could be dressed properly, disciplined strictly, and instructed in the truths of heaven and earth? What can you do for the child in this way?"

"I can teach the child what I have learned from this," replied Hester Prynne, laying her finger on the scarlet letter.

"Woman, it is your badge of shame!" the stern magistrate replied. "It is because of the stain which that letter indicates that we would put the child in other hands."

"Nevertheless," said the mother calmly, though growing more pale, "this badge has taught me—it teaches me daily—it is teaching me at this moment—lessons that would serve the child well."

"We will judge carefully," said Bellingham. "Good Master Wilson, I pray you, examine this Pearl and see whether she has had such Christian upbringing as is fitting for a child of her age."

The old minister seated himself in an armchair and attempted to draw Pearl closer to him.

The child, unaccustomed to the touch of anyone but her mother, pulled away. She escaped through the open window and stood on the upper step, looking like a wild, tropical bird ready to take flight into the upper air. Mr. Wilson was astonished at this outbreak, for he was a grandfatherly sort of person and a favorite of children. He tried, however, to proceed with the examination.

"Pearl," he said solemnly, "you must listen carefully to your Christian instruction. Can you tell me, my child, who made you?"

Now Pearl knew well enough who made her, for Hester had begun her child's Christian education as soon as was proper. But that perversity, which all children have some of and which little Pearl had tenfold of, now took hold of her. After many ungracious refusals to answer good Mr. Wilson's question, the child finally announced she had not been made at all. Rather, she had been plucked by her mother off the bush of wild roses that grew by the prison door.

This fantasy was probably suggested by the governor's red roses, which grew near where she stood, and by the recollection of the prison rosebush, which she had passed on her way to the governor's mansion.

Old Roger Chillingworth, with a smile on his face, whispered something in the young clergyman's ear. Hester Prynne looked at the physician and was startled to perceive the change that had come over his features—how much uglier they were—how his dark complexion seemed to have grown even duskier, and his figure more misshapen—since the days when she had lived with him. She met his eyes for an instant, but her attention was immediately called back to the fate of little Pearl.

"This is awful!" cried the governor, slowly recovering from the astonishment into which Pearl's response had thrown him. "Here is a child of three years old, yet she cannot tell who made her! Obviously, she is equally ignorant of her soul and what may become of it! Clearly, gentlemen, we need examine this question no further."

Hester caught hold of Pearl and drew her into her arms, confronting the old Puritan magistrate with a fierce expression. Alone in the world with this sole treasure to keep her heart alive, she felt she had the right to keep Pearl and was ready to defend that right to the death.

"God gave me the child!" she cried. "He gave her in exchange for all that you took from me. She is my happiness!—she is my torture, nonetheless! Pearl keeps me here in life! She punishes me, too! You will not take her! I will die first!"

"My poor woman," said the not unkind old minister, "the child will be well cared for—far better than you can do it."

"God gave her into my keeping," repeated Hester, her voice rising almost to a shriek. "I will not give her up!" And here, by sudden impulse, she turned to the young clergyman, Mr. Dimmesdale. "Speak for me!" she cried. "You were my minister and had charge of my soul. You know me better than these men can. I will not lose the child! Speak for me! You know what is in my heart! I will not lose the child! See to it!"

At this wild appeal, the young minister stepped forward. He was pale and held his hand over his heart, as was his custom whenever his peculiarly nervous temperament was thrown into agitation. He looked more careworn and emaciated than he had three years before when he spoke to Hester as she stood on the scaffold. Whether it was his failing health, or whatever the cause might be, his large dark eyes had a world of pain in their troubled and melancholy depth.

"There is truth in what she says," began the minister, in a voice sweet and tremulous, but powerful enough to echo in the hall, "—truth in what Hester says and in the feeling which inspires her! God gave her the child. He also gave her an instinctive knowledge of its nature and requirements. And, moreover, is there not a quality of sacredness in the relation between this mother and this child?"

"What are you saying, good Master Dimmesdale?" interrupted the governor. "Make yourself clear, I pray you!"

"We must let her keep the child," resumed

the minister. "For, if we decide otherwise, do we not say that the Heavenly Father makes light of her sin? And do we not say that there is no distinction between unhallowed lust and holy love? This child of its father's guilt and its mother's shame has come from the hand of God. God has sent it as a blessing, the one blessing in her life. But he has also sent it as a punishment, an ongoing reminder of her sinful act. Look at how she has dressed the child, as a reminder of that red symbol that sears her breast."

"Well said!" cried good Mr. Wilson. "I had feared the woman was ridiculing the symbol by dressing the child this way!"

"Not so! Not so!" continued Mr. Dimmesdale. "She recognizes the solemn miracle which God has wrought in the existence of that child. And she may feel too that this gift was meant to keep the mother's soul alive and preserve her from the blacker depths of sin into which Satan might have sought to plunge her! For Hester Prynne's sake and for the poor child's sake, let us leave them as Providence has seen fit to place them!"

"You speak, my friend, with a strange earnestness," said old Roger Chillingworth, smiling at him.

"And there is great significance to his words," added the Reverend Mr. Wilson. "What do you say, worshipful Master Bellingham? Has he not pleaded well for this poor woman?"

"He has, indeed," answered the magistrate. "We will leave the matter as it now stands, provided there is no further scandal associated with the woman. However, at the proper time, the child must prove her knowledge in the catechism to you or Master Dimmesdale. Furthermore, when she is old enough, she must attend school and church."

The young minister withdrew a few steps and stood with his face partially concealed by the heavy fold of the curtain. Pearl, that wild and flighty little elf, stole softly toward him and, taking his hand in the grasp of both her own, laid her cheek against it. The caress was so tender that Hester had to ask herself, "Is that my Pearl?" The minister looked around, laid his hand on the child's head, hesitated an instant, then kissed her brow.

Little Pearl's unexpected mood of sentiment lasted no longer. She laughed and went capering down the hall. Indeed, she moved so airily that old Mr. Wilson raised a question whether even her tiptoes touched the floor.

"The little baggage has witchcraft in her, I'd swear," he said to Mr. Dimmesdale. "She does not need an old woman's broomstick to fly!"

"A strange child!" remarked old Roger Chillingworth. "It is easy to see her mother in her. Would it be possible, do you think, to analyze the child's nature and, from that, make a shrewd guess at the father?"

"No, that would be a distortion of the proper use of the intellect," said Mr. Wilson. "Better to leave the mystery as we find it, unless Providence reveals it of its own accord. That way, every good Christian man has the right to show a father's kindness toward the poor, deserted babe."

The business now concluded, Hester Prynne and Pearl left the governor's mansion. As they descended the steps, it is said that a chamber window was thrown open; from that window, and forth into the sunny day, was thrust the face of Mistress Hibbins, Governor Bellingham's ill-tempered sister. This is the same Mistress Hibbins who, a few years later, was executed as a witch.

"Hist! Hist!" she said, while her ill-omened features seemed to cast a shadow over the cheerfulness and newness of the house. "Will you go with us tonight? There will be a merry company in the forest. And I practically promised the Black Man that pretty Hester Prynne would join the company."

"You'll have to make up an excuse for me to him," answered Hester, with a triumphant smile. "I must stay at home and keep watch over my little Pearl. Had they taken her from me, I would have willingly gone into the forest with you and signed my name in the Black Man's book with my own blood."

"We shall have you there soon!" said the witch lady, frowning as she drew back her head.

If we suppose that such an exchange really took place, we could say that it illustrated the young minister's argument for why Hester must keep the child. Clearly, the child saved her from Satan's snare.

CHAPTER 9

The Leech

Under the name of Roger Chillingworth, it will be remembered, was hidden another name which was never to be spoke again. When he had first arrived in Boston three years earlier, he had emerged from the wilderness and captivity expecting to rejoin his wife in the warmth and cheerfulness of a home. Instead, he saw that woman standing upon the scaffold with an infant in her arms, the very model of sin. It is no surprise that he chose not to be associated with the contagion of her dishonor. There had been rumors that he lay at the bottom of the ocean. So he chose to let others believe that was the case and became Roger Chillingworth. Only Hester knew the truth—and he held the lock and key to her silence.

With Roger Chillingworth's new life grew a new and dark purpose. He settled in Boston. His learning and his intelligence had made him well acquainted with medical science. Physicians were uncommon in the New World, so the community welcomed a man of such knowledge and skill. His time as a captive of the Indians, in addition, had acquainted him with the medicinal properties of native herbs and roots.

The learned Roger Chillingworth appeared to be concerned that he live a proper religious life. Soon after his arrival in Boston, he chose the Reverend Mr. Dimmesdale for his spiritual guide. About this time, the health of Mr. Dimmesdale had begun to fail. Many felt that this was the result of his being too earnestly devoted to his pastoral duties and to his frequent fasts and vigils. He himself, on the other hand, said with characteristic humility, that if Providence should see fit to remove him, it would be because of his own unworthiness to carry out his duties here on earth. Whatever the case, he grew emaciated. His voice, though still rich and sweet, had a certain melancholy echo of decay in it. He was often observed, when surprised, to put his hand over his heart, as if reacting to pain.

Given Mr. Dimmesdale's failing health, many in the community felt that it must be the hand of Providence that brought such a skilled physician as Roger Chillingworth at this time. Some even suggested that Heaven had wrought a miracle, transporting an eminent physician from a German university bodily through the air and setting him down at the door of Mr. Dimmesdale's study.

Roger Chillingworth quickly took a strong interest in the young clergyman. He expressed his alarm at his pastor's state of health and was anxious to attempt a cure. The other members of the congregation urged the minister to accept the physician's offer. Mr. Dimmesdale, however, gently repelled their pleas.

"I need no medicine," he said.

His condition continued to worsen. His face grew paler and thinner each week. It became his constant habit to hold his hand over his heart. The elders of the church pressed him harder to accept the aid that Providence so clearly offered him. Finally, he promised to consult with the physician.

"Were it God's will," said the Reverend Mr. Dimmesdale when he first met with Roger Chillingworth for medical advice, "I could be content that my labors and sins should soon end. I could be content that my body be buried in my grave and my spirit go to whatever awaits it."

"Ah," replied Roger Chillingworth quietly, "young men give up their hold of life so easily! Saintly men are so ready to walk the golden pavements of Heaven."

"No," answered the young minister, putting his hand to his heart, "if I were worthy to walk there, I could be more content to do my work here."

"Good men always see themselves as unworthy," said the physician.

Thus, the mysterious old Roger Chillingworth became the medical advisor of the Reverend Mr. Dimmesdale. Gradually, the two men began to spend much time together. For the sake of the minister's health and to allow the leech to gather plants with healing balm in them, they took long walks on the seashore or in the forest. As they walked, their talk mingled with the plash and murmur of the waves and the solemn wind-anthem among the treetops. Or they would have long, philosophical discussions in the study of one or the other of the men. The minister felt as if his eyes were being opened to new worlds in his conversations with this man of science. But he could not tolerate such exposure for long, and quickly retreated into the limits of what the church defined as orthodox.

Roger Chillingworth studied his patient carefully. He felt it essential to know the man before attempting to do him good. In Arthur Dimmesdale, thought and imagination were so active and intense that it seemed likely that physical illness would have its root there. So Roger Chillingworth strove to go deep into his patient's heart, digging among his principles, prying into his recollections, and probing every thing with a cautious touch, like a treasure seeker in a dark cavern.

As time went on, the two men came to discuss the whole sphere of human thought and study. But no secret, such as the physician imagined must exist, ever stole out of the minister's consciousness into his companion's ear.

After a time, and at the suggestion of Roger Chillingworth, the two men came to be lodged in the same house. They each took rooms in a pious widow's house. In this way, the physician could better study his patient and attempt to help him. Mr. Dimmesdale's apartment was in the front of the house with a sunny exposure. Here the minister piled up his library. On the other side of the house, old Roger Chillingworth arranged his study and a laboratory where he could compound drugs and chemicals. His work in alchemy had given him skill in such activities. In this situation, these two learned men settled; each had his own domain, yet they passed freely from one apartment to the other, expressing their interest in each other's work.

Many continued to feel that Providence had brought the physician to the ailing minister. But gradually, some took a different view. A few hinted that possibly, during his Indian captivity, Chillingworth had joined with the savage priests in their incantations; he had, they suggested, learned powers of enchantment and black arts. Many more people, however, agreed that Chillingworth's physical appearance had undergone a significant change since he came to Boston. At first, his expression had been calm, meditative, scholar-like. Now, there was something ugly and evil in his face, which they had not previously noticed. Some suggested that the fire in his laboratory had been brought from the lower regions and was fed by infernal fuel; and so, as might be expected, his face was getting sooty with the smoke.

To sum up the matter, it became the opinion of many that the Reverend Arthur Dimmesdale was haunted either by Satan himself or Satan's emissary in the appearance of old Roger Chillingworth. They were sure, however, that this diabolical agent had the Divine permission to test the soul of the minister. And they were even more sure that the minister would triumph. The people looked, with unshaken hope, to see the minister come forth from the conflict, transfigured with the glory, which he would unquestionably win.

But, to judge from the gloom and terror in the depths of the poor minister's eyes, the battle was a difficult one, and the victory far from certain.

CHAPTER 10

The Leech and His Patient

Old Roger Chillingworth, throughout life, had been calm and kindly in temperament. Though he had not shown warm affections, he had been a pure and upright man in all his dealings with the world. He had begun his investigation with the integrity of a judge, looking only for truth. But, as he proceeded, a terrible fascination took hold of him. He now dug into the poor clergyman's heart like a miner searching for gold—or, rather, like a robber delving into a grave in search of a jewel that had been buried with the dead man.

Sometimes, a light glimmered out of the physician's eyes, burning blue and ominous, like the reflections of a furnace. It was as if the soil where this dark miner was working had possibly shown some indications that encouraged him.

"This man," he said to himself at one such moment, "pure and spiritual as he seems, has inherited a strong animal nature from his father or mother. Let us dig a little further in the direction of this vein!"

Then, after a long and fruitless search into the minister's dim interior, the physician would turn back, discouraged, and begin his quest toward another point. He groped along as stealthily and cautiously as a thief entering a chamber where a man lies only half-asleep, seeking the very treasure that the man guards with great care. Once in a while his careful movements would disturb the sleeper. But on those rare occasions when the minister felt a hint of suspicion, he would turn his startled eyes toward the physician; all the minister would see was his kind, watchful, sympathizing, but never intrusive friend.

Often their discussions would be carried out in the physician's laboratory, while the old man extracted some potent drugs from leaves he had collected in the forest. One such day, leaning his forehead on his hand, and his elbow on the sill of the open window that looked out toward the graveyard, the minister talked with Roger Chillingworth. The old man was examining a bundle of ugly plants.

"Where," he asked, glancing at the bundle,

"where, my kind doctor, did you gather herbs with such dark, flabby leaves?"

"In the graveyard that you see outside the window," the physician answered, continuing his work. "They are new to me. I found them growing on a grave that had no tombstone. They look as if they grew out of the dead man's heart; it may be that some hideous secret was buried with him and that he would have been better off to confess it during his lifetime."

"Perhaps," said Mr. Dimmesdale, "he desired to do so but could not."

"And what did his silence gain him?" asked the physician. "These black weeds have sprung out of the buried heart to make the crime known."

"That, good sir, is just a fantasy of yours," replied the minister. "There is nothing that can draw forth the secrets that may be buried with a human heart. Such secrets will not be revealed until the Day of Judgment. And such revelation will be a relief to that heart."

"Then why not reveal them here?" asked Roger Chillingworth. "Why shouldn't those wracked with guilt take advantage of such relief in life?"

"They mostly do," the clergyman said, pressing his hand to his heart. "Many a poor soul has given its confidence to me in the prime of life as well as on the deathbed. And always, after such a confession, I have witnessed the great relief felt by those sinful brothers and sisters. And why not? Why should a wretched man, guilty, say, of murder, prefer to keep the dead corpse buried in his own heart, rather than fling it forth at once and let the universe take care of it!"

"Yet some men bury their secrets," observed the calm physician.

"True, there are such men," answered Dimmesdale. "Perhaps they feel that, once their evil has been revealed, they will no longer be able to achieve good in the world. To their own unutterable torment, they go among their fellow creatures, looking pure as new-fallen snow; meanwhile, their hearts are speckled and spotted with the evil of which they cannot rid themselves."

"These men deceive themselves," said Roger Chillingworth. "If they seek to glorify God, let them not lift heavenward their unclean hands! Would you have me believe, oh pious friend, that a false show can be better—can do more for God's glory and man's welfare—than God's own truth? Trust me, such men deceive themselves."

"It may be so," said the young clergyman, sounding indifferent. He was about to change the topic when their conversation was interrupted by the clear, wild laughter of a young child's voice from the adjacent burial ground. Looking out the window, the minister saw Hester Prynne and little Pearl passing along the footpath that crossed the cemetery.

Pearl looked as beautiful as the day. But she was in one of those moods of perverse merriment that seemed to remove her entirely out of the sphere of sympathy or human contact. She skipped irreverently from one grave to another. Then, coming to a broad, flat tombstone, she began to dance upon it. Hester commanded and urged her to act more appropriately. In reply, little Pearl paused to gather the prickly burrs from a tall weed that grew beside the tomb. Taking a handful of these, she arranged them along the lines of the scarlet letter that decorated her mother's dress. The burrs stuck tenaciously to the material; Hester did not pluck them off.

Roger Chillingworth had by now approached the window and smiled grimly down.

"There is no respect for authority, no sense of right or wrong in that child," he remarked, half to himself. The other day, I saw her spatter the governor himself with water at the cattle-trough in Spring Lane. Is the imp altogether evil? Does she feel any affection?"

"Whether she is capable of good or not, I don't know," Dimmesdale said in a quiet way, as if he had been discussing the point with himself.

Looking up at the window with a bright but naughty smile, Pearl threw one of the burrs at the Reverend Mr. Dimmesdale. The sensitive clergyman shrank with nervous dread from the missile.

Seeing his reaction, Pearl clapped her little hands in extravagant ecstasy. Hester looked up and all four people regarded one another in silence for a moment. Then the child laughed and shouted, "Come away, Mother! Come away or the Black Man will catch you! He has got hold of the minister already. Come away, or he will catch you! But he cannot catch little Pearl!"

So she drew her mother away, skipping, dancing, and frisking fantastically among the hillocks of the dead people. She was like a creature that had no connection with the human world of the living or the dead. It was as if she had been made out of new elements, a law unto herself.

"There goes a woman," resumed Roger Chillingworth, after a pause, "whose sin is hidden from no one. Is Hester Prynne less miserable, do you think, because of that scarlet letter on her breast?"

"I truly believe it," answered the clergyman. "However, I cannot answer for her. But I must think it is better for the sufferer to show his pain, as this poor woman Hester does, than to cover it all up in his heart."

There was another pause. The physician turned back to his examination of the plants he had gathered.

"But now," the Reverend Dimmesdale said, "I must ask whether you think, in truth, my health has improved any from your kindly care. Please speak frankly, no matter how good or bad the situation is."

"The disorder is a strange one," said the physician, still busy with his plants. "Watching you every day, I would say you are very ill, but not so ill that a careful physician would have difficulty curing you. But—I am not sure what to say—the disease is what I seem to know, yet know it not."

"You speak in riddles, learned sir," said the pale minister.

"Then, to speak more plainly," continued the physician, "let me ask you this, my friend: Have all of the details of your disease been fully presented to me?"

"How can you ask that?" asked the minister. "Only a fool would call in a physician and then hide the sore!"

"You are saying, then, that nothing has been kept from me?" said Roger Chillingworth, fixing an eye, bright with intense and concentrated intelligence, on the minister's face. "Be it so! A bodily disease, which we look at as whole and entire within itself, may, after all, be just a symptom of some ailment in the spiritual part. But I hope you do not take any offense at my words."

"Then I need ask no further," said the clergyman, rising hastily from his chair. "You do not deal, I take it, in medicine for the soul!"

"Thus, a sickness," continued Roger Chillingworth, ignoring the interruption, "a sickness in your spirit shows itself in your body. But you want your physician to heal your bodily trouble? How can this be, unless you first lay open to him the wound or trouble in your soul?"

The physician was now standing, his low, dark, and misshapen figure confronting the emaciated and white-cheeked minister.

"No! Not to you—not to any earthly physician!" cried Mr. Dimmesdale passionately and turning his eyes, full and bright, and with a kind of fierceness, on old Roger Chillingworth. "Not to you! If my soul is diseased, then I put myself in the hands of the Physician of the soul. At His pleasure, He can cure or He can kill! Let Him do with me as He shall see fit. But who are you to meddle in this matter? Who are you to dare to thrust himself between the sufferer and his God?"

With a frantic gesture, he rushed out of the room.

"It is well to have taken this step," said Roger Chillingworth to himself, looking after the minister with a grave smile. "There is nothing lost. We will be friends again soon enough. But mark how passion has taken hold of this man. As with one passion, so with another! He has done a wild thing before now, this pious Mr. Dimmesdale, in the hot passion of his heart!"

It was not difficult to reestablish the relationship between the two companions. The young clergyman quickly realized his fit of temper had been inappropriate. He had, after all, asked the physician's advice. The kind old man had only been responding to his question. Before long, the physician resumed his medical supervision of the minister, doing his best for him. But each time Roger Chillingworth left the clergyman's apartment, he had a mysterious and puzzled smile on his lips. This expression was invisible in Mr. Dimmesdale's presence, but grew strongly evident as the physician crossed the threshold.

"A rare case!" he muttered. "I must look deeper into it. There is a strange sympathy between soul and body here!"

Not many days later, the Reverend Dimmesdale fell asleep while reading in his apartment at midday. The deep, deep slumber came over him, unawares as he sat in his chair. The depth of his sleep was so profound that he stirred not in his chair when old Roger Chillingworth entered the room. The physician advanced directly in front of his patient, laid his hand on the sleeping man's chest, and thrust aside the minister's shirt.

At that moment, Mr. Dimmesdale shuddered and slightly stirred.

After a brief pause, the physician turned away.

But with what a wild look of wonder, joy, and horror! With what ghastly rapture, too strong to be expressed with just the eyes and the face; and therefore bursting forth through the whole ugliness of his figure—making itself even riotously shown by the extravagant gestures with which he threw up his arms toward the ceiling and stamped his foot on the floor! If any man had seen old Roger Chillingworth at that moment of his ecstasy, he would have known how Satan reacts when a wicked human soul is lost to heaven and won into his kingdom.

But what distinguished the physician's ecstasy from Satan's was the hint of wonder in it!

CHAPTER 11

The Interior of a Heart

After the physician's discovery of the minister's secret, the relationship between the two men appeared to continue just as it had been. But, underneath, it changed significantly. The path was now clear to Roger Chillingworth. Calm, gentle, passionless as he appeared, there was now a quiet depth of malice in the unfortunate old man. He now came to imagine a more vicious revenge than any mortal had ever taken on an enemy. He made himself the one trusted friend so that all of the minister's remorse and agony would be revealed to him, the Pitiless, the Unforgiving!

Thus, Roger Chillingworth became much more than just an observer of the minister. He had access to the minister's interior world. He could play upon the man's conscience as he wished. As if by waving a magician's wand, he could maᴋe a thousand grisly phantoms rise up, flocking about the clergyman and pointing with their fingers at his heart. But the old man worked with a subtlety so perfect that the minister could never gain knowledge of the source of his discomfort.

The Reverend Dimmesdale sometimes felt as if there were some evil influence watching over him. He sometimes looked with fearful suspicion—even, at times, with horror and the bitterness of hatred—on the misshapen old physician. But he could find no cause for his feelings in the old man's words or actions, so he would conclude they must come from the evil secret that lay in his own heart. In an attempt to overcome these unchristian thoughts within himself, he would work even harder to strengthen his social familiarity with the old man.

While suffering under bodily disease, while tortured by some black trouble of the soul, and while under the sinister schemes of his deadliest enemy, the Reverend Mr. Dimmesdale had achieved brilliant popularity in his sacred work. The people found his voice like that of the angels; his words showed he understood their own sinful natures; his heart vibrated in unison with theirs and received their pain into itself. They believed him to be a miracle of holiness. They fancied him the mouthpiece of Heaven's messages of wisdom, reprimand, and love. To them, the very ground he walked upon was sacred.

It is inconceivable, the agony with which this public admiration tortured him! He longed to speak out the truth from his own pulpit and tell people what he was. "I, your pastor, whom you so reverence and trust, am utterly a pollution and a lie!"

More than once, he had gone into the pulpit, vowing not to come down until he had spoken such words. More than once, he had cleared his throat and drawn in the long, deep, and trembling breath, which, when sent forth again, would carry the burden of the black secret of his soul. More than once, he had actually spoken! Spoken! But how? He had told his hearers that he was altogether vile, the worst of sinners, an abomination. Could there be plainer speech than this?

Would not the people start up from their seats and tear him down out of the pulpit which he defiled? Not so, indeed! They heard it all, but only respected him more. "The godly youth!" they said among themselves. "The saint on earth! If he sees such sinfulness in his own pure soul, what a horrid sight would he see in mine!"

The minister well knew how his confession would be viewed. He had tried to soothe his soul by revealing his own guilty conscience—but he knew the people would only see him as all the purer for it. And so he added the knowledge of his own hypocrisy to his already burdened heart. He had spoken the truth and transformed it into a falsehood. But in his very nature, he loved the truth and loathed the lie. Therefore, above all things else, he loathed his miserable self!

His inward trouble drove him to extreme practices. In Mr. Dimmesdale's secret closet, under lock and key, there was a bloody scourge. Often, he had beaten himself about the shoulders with it. He laughed bitterly as he did so, and then beat himself even more pitilessly because of the bitter laughter. And he would often fast as an act of penance until his knees trembled beneath him.

Frequently, he kept vigils, night after night. In these long vigils, his brain often reeled and visions seemed to flit before him. He would see them faintly in the remote dimness of his room or more vividly and close beside him as he gazed at himself in his mirror. Now it was a herd of diabolic shapes that grinned and mocked the pale minister and beckoned him away with them. Now a group of shining angels who flew upward heavily, as if weighted down by sorrow. Now came the dead friends of his youth, and his white-bearded father, with a saint-like frown, and his mother, turning her face away as she passed by. And now, through the room which these spectral thoughts had made so ghastly, glided Hester

Prynne, leading along little Pearl and pointing her forefinger, first, at the scarlet letter on her breast, and then at the clergyman's own breast.

By an effort of his will, he could convince himself that these visions were not solid in their nature. They were not like the carved oaken table or the leather-bound book that lay on it. But even so, they were, in one sense, the truest and most substantial things that the poor minister now dealt with. The unspeakable misery of a life so false steals the substance out of the realities around us. To the untrue man, the whole universe is false—it shrinks to nothing within his grasp. And he himself becomes a shadow or, indeed, ceases to exist. The only truth that continued to give Mr. Dimmesdale a real existence on this earth was the anguish of his inmost soul.

On one of those ugly nights, the minister started from his chair. A new thought had struck him. There might be a moment's peace in it. Dressing himself if he were going to lead public worship, he stole softly down the steps, unbolted the door, and stepped into the lane.

CHAPTER 12

The Minister's Vigil

Mr. Dimmesdale moved through the sleeping town as if he were walking in the shadow of a dream. Soon he reached the spot where, seven years earlier, Hester had stood through her first hour of public shame. The same scaffold remained standing beneath the balcony of the meetinghouse. Seven long years of storm and sunshine had left the platform black and weather-stained. The steps were worn from the feet of many culprits who had ascended them since Hester did. The minister went up the steps.

It was a dark night in early May. A thick layer of clouds muffled the whole expanse of sky. It was so dark that, had the same crowd that witnessed Hester's punishment stood now before the scaffold, they would not have been able to see the minister. But all the town was asleep. There was no danger of discovery. The minister might stand there, if he wished, until morning glowed red in the east without risk.

Why had he come here? Did he wish to make a mockery of penitence? Or was it merely his own soul, which mocked itself? Remorse and cowardice had driven this poor, miserable man here to stand in the place of public shame at an hour when no one would see him there.

And so, while standing on the scaffold in this meaningless show of repentance, Mr. Dimmesdale was overcome with a great horror of mind, as if the universe were gazing at a scarlet token on his naked breast, right over his heart. In truth, there had long been the gnawing and poisonous tooth of bodily pain.

Without any effort of his will or power to restrain himself, he shrieked aloud. The outcry went pealing through the night and was beaten back from one house to another and reverberated from the hills in the background. It was as if a company of devils, sensing so much misery in it, had made a plaything of the sound and were tossing it to and fro.

"It is done!" muttered the minister, covering his face with his hands. "The whole town will awake and hurry forth and find me here!"

But it was not so. The shriek must have sounded far louder to his own ears than it actually was. The town did not awake. Or, if it did, the drowsy slumberers mistook the cry for something frightful in a dream—or else for the noise of witches, whose voices were often heard to pass over the settlements as they rode with Satan through the air.

Dimmesdale slowly uncovered his eyes and looked about. He saw Governor Bellingham's mansion at some distance. At one of the bedroom windows, he saw the old magistrate himself with a lamp in his hand, wearing a long white nightshirt. He looked like a ghost, called forth from the grave. The cry had apparently startled him.

At another window of the same house stood old Mistress Hibbins, the governor's sister, also with a lamp. She thrust her sour and discontented face forth from the window and looked anxiously upward. Beyond a shadow of a doubt, this respected witch lady had heard Dimmesdale's outcry with its echoes and reverberations. She had interpreted it as the clamor of the fiends and night-hags with whom she was well known to make excursions into the forest. Seeing the gleam of Governor Bellingham's lamp, the old lady quickly extinguished her own and vanished. Possibly, she went up among the clouds. The magistrate peered blindly out into the darkness for another moment and then, able to see nothing, retired from the window.

The minister grew calm. His eyes were soon greeted by a little, glimmering light a long way off. As it gradually approached, it momentarily illuminated familiar objects—here a garden fence, and there a latticed window-pane, here a pump with its full trough of water, and there an arched oak door with an iron knocker. The Reverend Mr. Dimmesdale noted all of these details as the light came ever closer. Now he heard footsteps and knew that the gleam of the lantern would soon fall upon him and reveal his long-hidden secret.

As the light drew nearer, he saw within its illuminated circle his brother clergyman, the Reverend Mr. Wilson. Mr. Dimmesdale suspected that Mr. Wilson had been praying at the bedside of some dying man. And so he had. The good old minister came freshly from the death-chamber of Governor Winthrop, who had passed from earth to heaven within that very hour. The good Father Wilson was going homeward, aiding his footsteps with a lantern. To Dimmesdale, it seemed as if the Reverend Mr. Wilson were surrounded with a radiant halo that glorified him amid this gloomy night of sin. Such a thought made Mr. Dimmesdale smile and almost laugh—and then wonder if he were going mad.

The Reverend Mr. Wilson passed beside the scaffold, closely muffling his great cloak about him with one arm and holding the lantern before him with the other. As he came close, Mr. Dimmesdale could hardly restrain himself from speaking.

"Good evening to you, Father Wilson! Come up here, I pray you, and pass a pleasant hour with me!"

Good Heavens! Had Mr. Dimmesdale actually spoken? For an instant, he believed those words had actually passed his lips. But they were uttered only within his imagination. The Reverend Mr. Wilson continued to step slowly onward, looking carefully at the muddy path before his feet, never once turning his head toward the guilty platform. When his light had faded in the distance, Mr. Dimmesdale realized from the faintness he felt that the last few moments had been a crisis of terrible anxiety. But his mind had also felt a kind of lurid playfulness.

Shortly afterward, the same grisly sense of the humorous again stole in among the solemn phantoms of his thought. He felt his legs growing stiff with unaccustomed chilliness of the night air. He began to doubt whether he would be able to descend the steps of the scaffold. Morning would break and some early riser would come out and see him in the dim light. Word would spread and all the townspeople would come stumbling over their thresholds, turning up their amazed and horror-stricken faces around the scaffold. In the red eastern light they would see the Reverend Arthur Dimmesdale, half-frozen to death, overwhelmed with shame, standing where Hester Prynne had stood!

Carried away by the grotesque horror of this picture, the minister, without realizing it, burst into a great peal of laughter. It was immediately responded to by a light, airy, childish laugh. With a thrill of the heart, he recognized the tones of little Pearl.

"Pearl! Little Pearl!" he cried. Then, lowering his voice, he said, "Hester! Hester Prynne! Are you there?"

"Yes, it is Hester Prynne," she replied in a tone of surprise. "And my little Pearl is with me."

The minister heard her footsteps approaching the scaffold. "Where are you coming from, Hester? What brings you here at this hour?"

"I have been watching at a deathbed," answered Hester Prynne. "At Governor Winthrop's deathbed. I have taken his measure for a burial robe and am going home to my cottage."

"Come up here, Hester—you and little Pearl," said the Reverend Mr. Dimmesdale. "You have both been here before, but I was not with you. Come up here once again, and we will all three stand together!"

She silently ascended the steps and stood on the platform, holding little Pearl by the hand. The minister took the child's other hand. The moment he did so, he felt what seemed like a tumultuous rush of new life pouring like a torrent into his heart. It was as if the mother and child were communicating their vital warmth into the numbness of his soul. The three formed an electric chain.

"Minister!" whispered little Pearl.

"What is it, child?" asked Mr. Dimmesdale.

"Will you stand here with mother and me tomorrow at noontime?" asked Pearl.

"No, my little Pearl!" answered the minister. With the new energy of the moment, all the dread of public exposure had returned to him. "No, my child. I shall, indeed, stand with your mother and you one day, but not tomorrow!"

Pearl laughed and attempted to pull her hand away, but the minister held it fast.

"A moment longer, my child!" he said.

"But will you not promise," asked Pearl, "to take my hand and my mother's hand tomorrow at noontime?"

"Not then, Pearl," said the minister, "but another time!"

"What other time?" pestered the child.

"At the great judgment day!" whispered the minister. "Then, before the judgment seat, your mother, you, and I must stand together. But the daylight of this world shall not see our meeting!"

Pearl laughed again.

Before Mr. Dimmesdale had finished speaking,

a light gleamed far and wide over the muffled sky, doubtless caused by a meteor. So powerful was its radiance that it completely illuminated the dense layer of clouds that hung between earth and stars. The great vault of the sky brightened, like the dome of a lamp. It showed the familiar scene of the street with the distinctness of midday—but also with the awfulness that unusual light gives objects. The wooden houses with their gable peaks; the doorsteps and thresholds, with the early grass springing up about them; the gardens, black with freshly turned earth—all were visible, but with an unusual appearance that seemed to give another moral interpretation to them than they had ever borne before.

And there stood the minister, with his hand over his heart; and Hester Prynne, with the embroidered letter glimmering on her breast; and little Pearl, herself a symbol and the connecting link between those two. They stood in the noon of that strange and solemn splendor. It seemed as if the light were meant to reveal all secrets, and were the daybreak that shall unite all who belong with another.

There was witchcraft in little Pearl's eyes. Her face wore that strange smile that so often made its expression so elvish. She withdrew her hand from Mr. Dimmesdale's and pointed across the street. But he clasped both his hands over his breast and cast his eyes toward the sky.

It was common in those days to interpret the appearance of a meteor as a revelation from a supernatural force. Sometimes it signaled Indian warfare; sometimes pestilence. Usually, the interpretation rested on the observation of a single eyewitness who beheld the wonder through the colored, magnifying, and distorting medium of his imagination and shaped it more distinctly in his afterthought.

In this case, the disease in the minister's own eye and heart led him to behold the appearance of an immense letter—the letter A—marked out in lines of dull red light. The meteor may have shown itself at that moment burning duskily through the veil of cloud. But it probably had no such shape as his guilty imagination gave it.

There was an unusual circumstance that affected Mr. Dimmesdale's psychological state at this moment. All the time he gazed up at the sky, he was aware that little Pearl was pointing her finger toward old Roger Chillingworth.

The deformed man was standing not far from the scaffold. The meteoric light gave a new appearance to his features. It revealed the malevolence with which he looked upon his victim. Roger Chillingworth might have passed as the archfiend, standing there on judgment day, waiting to claim the soul of the minister.

The meteor vanished and it seemed as if the street and all else was annihilated. But so vivid was the expression of the old alchemist that the minister believed it was still visible, as if painted on the darkness.

"Who is that man, Hester?" gasped Mr. Dimmesdale, overcome with terror. "I tremble to see him. Do you know who he really is? I hate him, Hester!"

She remembered her oath and was silent.

"I tell you, my soul shivers at the sight of him," muttered the minister. "Who is he? Can you not help me? I have a nameless horror of the man."

"Minister," said little Pearl, "I can tell you who he is!"

"Quick, then, child!" said the minister bending his ear close to her lips.

Pearl mumbled something into his ear. It sounded like human language but was only such gibberish as children amuse themselves with. If it involved any secret information about old Roger Chillingworth, it was in a tongue that the minister could not understand. The elfish child then laughed aloud.

"Do you mock me?" said the minister.

"You were not bold! You were not true!" answered the child. "You would not promise to take my hand and my mother's hand tomorrow at noontime."

"Worthy sir," said the physician, advancing to the foot of the platform. "Pious Master

Dimmesdale! Is it really you? Well, well. We men of study need to be looked after carefully. We dream in our waking moments and walk in our sleep. Come, my dear friend, and let me lead you home."

"How did you know I was here?" asked the minister fearfully.

"Truly, I did not know at all," answered Roger Chillingworth. "I spent most of the night at the bedside of Governor Winthrop, doing what I could to ease his pain. I was on my way home when this strange light shone out. Come with me, I beg you, or you will be too ill to give your sermon tomorrow."

"I will go with you," said Mr. Dimmesdale.

With an air of dejection, like one waking from an ugly dream, he joined the physician and was led away.

The next day, which was the Sabbath, he preached a sermon that people said was the richest and most powerful ever to come from his lips. It is said that many souls were brought to the path of truth by that powerful sermon. But, as the minister came down the pulpit steps, the gray-bearded sexton met him, holding up a black glove. The minister recognized it as his own.

"It was found," said the sexton, "this morning on the scaffold. Satan dropped it there, I imagine, as a vulgar joke against your reverence. But he was blind and foolish, as he ever is. A pure hand needs no glove to cover it."

"Thank you, my good friend," said the minister gravely. But he was startled at heart. So confused was his memory that he had almost thought of the events of the past night as a mere vision. "Yes, it seems to be my glove, indeed."

"Since Satan saw fit to steal it, your reverence will have to handle him without gloves from now on," remarked the old sexton, smiling grimly. "But did your reverence hear of the sign seen last night? A great red letter in the sky—the letter A—which we interpret to stand for Angel. Since our good Governor Winthrop was made an angel last night, it was fitting that there was such a sign."

"No," answered the minister. "I had not heard of it."

CHAPTER 13

Another View of Hester

In her recent meeting with Dimmesdale on the scaffold, Hester Prynne was shocked at his condition. His nerve seemed absolutely destroyed. His moral force was reduced to childish weakness. Knowing what she did of Roger Chillingworth, Hester could well imagine that something more than Mr. Dimmesdale's own conscience was gnawing at his heart and destroying his peace of mind. And, knowing what the minister had once been, she had been moved by his need for help against his secret enemy. She decided that he had a right to her support and aid. The links that had once united her to the rest of humankind had all been broken. But between her and Dimmesdale was the iron link of mutual crime which neither she nor he could ever break. Like all other ties, it brought with it its obligations.

Hester's relationship to her society had changed. Years had come and gone. Pearl was now seven years old. Her mother, with the scarlet letter glittering in its fantastic embroidery, had long been a familiar object to the townspeople. In their eyes, Hester had accepted her sentence humbly. She made no claim to the privileges of the blameless. What is more, she had justly earned a reputation as one who tirelessly helped the poor, the sick, the needy. In any household darkened with trouble or sickness, the embroidered letter glimmered like a candle of hope and comfort. Hester's nature showed itself warm and rich. She was a wellspring of human tenderness. The world now saw her as a Sister of Mercy. The letter had become a symbol of her calling. Such helpfulness was found in her—so much power to do and power to sympathize—that many people refused to interpret the scarlet A by its original meaning. They said it meant Able, so strong was Hester Prynne.

Hester never asked for gratitude for efforts. In fact, she avoided it. When sunshine came again to the house that had been darkened with trouble, Hester's shadow faded across the threshold. If she passed grateful townspeople in the street, she never raised her head to receive their greeting.

The rulers, and the wise and learned men of the community, took longer to acknowledge Hester's good qualities than did the townspeople in general. But eventually, day-by-day, their sour and rigid wrinkles relaxed into expressions of tolerant acceptance. Individuals in private life, however, went much further. They had not merely forgiven Hester. No, they had even begun to look upon the scarlet letter as a symbol, not of sin, but of Hester's many good deeds since. "Do you see that woman with the embroidered letter?" they would say to strangers. "It is our Hester—the town's own Hester—who is so kind to the poor, so helpful to the sick, so comforting to the afflicted!"

Then, of course, following the tendency of the worst of human nature, they would whisper of the black scandal in the past. But even so, the letter had the effect of the cross on a nun's snow-white collar. It bestowed on Hester a kind of sacredness that enabled her to walk safely amid all danger. Had she fallen among thieves it would have kept her safe. It was reported, and believed by many, that an Indian had drawn his arrow at her, but it had struck the letter and fallen harmlessly to the ground.

The effect of the scarlet letter on Hester Prynne, however, had been quite different. All the gracefulness of her character had withered up and fallen away, like the so many leaves. What was left was a bare and harsh outline. Even the attractiveness of her person had undergone a similar change, emphasized by the austerity of her clothing. Her rich and luxuriant hair was so completely hidden by a cap that not a shining lock of it ever once gushed into the sunshine. There seemed to be no longer in Hester's face anything for Love to dwell upon, nothing in her form that Passion would ever dream of embracing. But she who has ever once been a woman and ceased to be so might at any moment become a woman again, if there were only the magic touch to effect the transformation. We shall see whether Hester Prynne were ever afterward so touched and so transfigured.

But for all her coldness and distance, Hester was very much alive. The circumstances of her life had caused her to turn from passion and feeling to thought. And in her thinking, Hester was much more in tune with those Europeans whose newly emancipated intellect had overthrown the ancient prejudices and principles, than she was with the stern and unbending ideas of the early settlers in New England. In her lonesome cottage by the seashore, thoughts visited her such as dared enter no other dwelling in New England. Shadowy guests, that others would have seen as perilous demons, practically could have been seen knocking at her door.

It is always surprising that the boldest thinkers often conform the most completely to the external regulations of society. So it seemed to be with Hester. And well it was, for had she spoken out, she probably would have suffered death from the stern judges of the period for attempting to undermine the foundations of the Puritan establishment.

But when it came to little Pearl, Hester felt at a loss in how to educate the child. Everything was against the child. The world was hostile. The child's own nature had something wrong with it. Pearl was a constant reminder that she had been born out of Hester's lawless passion. Hester often asked herself, with a bitter heart, whether it was for ill or good that the poor little creature had been born at all.

Indeed, the same dark question often rose into her mind with reference to the whole race of womanhood. Was existence worth accepting, even to the happiest woman? The first step toward improvement would be to tear the whole system down and build it up anew. Then, the very nature of man must be essentially modified before woman would be allowed to assume what would seem like a fair and suitable position in the world. But such seemed too much, Hester thought, as she wandered in the dark labyrinth of mind. At times her doubt became so great that she wondered whether it would not be better to send Pearl to heaven at once and to commit herself to whatever fate Eternal Justice saw fit for her.

The scarlet letter had not succeeded in putting Hester Prynne on the path intended by those who had condemned her to wear it.

Her meeting with the Reverend Mr. Dimmesdale on the night of his vigil had given her more to think about. She had witnessed the intense misery beneath which the minister struggled. She saw that he stood on the verge of lunacy, it he had not already stepped across it. A secret enemy had been continually by his side, in the disguise of a friend and helper. She could not help but feel responsible for unleashing this fiend on the minister. At the time of her promise, she could see no choice but to accept Roger Chillingworth's scheme of disguise. It had seemed the only way to protect Dimmesdale from certain ruin. But her choice, it now seemed, had been the far worse alternative of the two. She made up her mind to redeem her error, if at all possible.

She no longer felt so inadequate to cope with Roger Chillingworth as she had on that night seven years ago when they had talked together in the prison chamber. She had climbed to a new level since then. The old man, on the other hand, had brought himself nearer to her level—or perhaps below it—by the revenge he had stooped for.

In short, Hester Prynne decided to meet her former husband and do whatever she could to rescue the victim who he held in his grip. It did not take her long to find an opportunity for such a meeting. One afternoon while walking with Pearl in a secluded part of the peninsula, she saw the old physician searching for roots and herbs to concoct his medicines with.

CHAPTER 14

Hester and the Physician

Hester told little Pearl to run down to the water's edge and play with the shells and tangled seaweed, while she talked with the gatherer of herbs. So the child flew away like a bird and, pulling off her shoes, went pattering along the moist margin of the sea. Here and there, she stopped and peeped curiously into a pool left by the tide as a mirror for Pearl to see her face in. Peeping out of the pool, with dark glistening curls and an elf-smile in her eyes, was the image of a little maid. Pearl, having no other playmate, invited the little maid to take her hand and run a race with her. But the visionary little figure in the water beckoned the same way, as if to say, "This is a better place! Come into the tidal pool!" Pearl, stepping in, saw her own white feet on the bottom. And, out of a still lower depth, came the gleam of a fragmentary smile, floating to and fro on the water.

Meanwhile, her mother had approached the physician.

"I would have a word with you," she said.

"Ah! Is it Mistress Hester who would have a word with old Roger Chillingworth?" he answered, raising himself from his stooping posture. "Certainly. You know, Mistress, I hear good news for you on all sides. Just yesterday evening, a wise and godly magistrate was speaking of you. He told me that there was debate in the council of whether or not to permit you to take the scarlet letter off. I promise you, Hester, I urged the worshipful magistrate that it be done immediately!"

"It is not up to the magistrates to take off this letter," replied Hester calmly. "Were I worthy of having it removed, it would fall away by its own nature or be transformed into some different symbol."

"Then wear it if you wish," he answered. "The letter is beautifully embroidered and suits you well."

As the physician spoke, Hester had been looking steadily at the old man. She was shocked to see what a change had come over him in the past seven years. It was not so much that he had grown older, for he still had a wiry vigor and alertness. But his former appearance of an intellectual and studious man, calm and quiet, had altogether vanished. It had been replaced by an eager, searching, almost fierce yet carefully guarded look. He tried to mask this expression with a smile; but the smile flickered over his face with such mockery that the observer could see his blackness all the better for it. Now and again a glare of red light seemed to come from his eyes. It was as if the old man's soul were on fire, smoldering duskily within his breast until some puff of passion blew it into momentary flame. He would smoother it as quickly as possible and attempt to look as if nothing of the kind had happened.

In a word, old Roger Chillingworth was clear evidence of man's potential for transforming himself into a devil, if he will only, for a period of time, do the devil's work. Seven years of devoted study of a heart full of torture and of adding fuel to that fiery torture had thus transformed the unhappy old man.

The scarlet letter burned on Hester Prynne's breast as she looked at the physician. Here was another ruin for which she was at least partly responsible.

"What do you see in my face that makes you look at me so earnestly?" asked Roger Chillingworth.

"Something that would make me weep, if there were any tears bitter enough for it," she replied. "But let that be. It is of your patient who is in such misery that I wish to speak."

"And what of him?" cried Roger Chillingworth eagerly, as if he loved the topic. "In truth, Mistress Hester, I was just now thinking of the gentleman. Speak freely."

"When we last spoke seven years ago," said Hester, "you forced a promise of secrecy from me. At the time, I had no choice but to be silent about your identity, as you requested. There was no other way for me to protect him. But I gave that pledge with the greatest misgiving. Since that day, no man is so near to him as you. You walk behind his every footstep. You are beside him every moment. You search his thoughts. You burrow and rankle in his heart! You cause him to die daily a living death—and he knows you not. In permitting this, I have acted falsely toward the only man to whom I could still be true!"

"What other choice did you have?" asked Roger Chillingworth. "Had I openly condemned this man, he would have been hurled from the pulpit into a dungeon—and from there, perhaps, to the gallows!"

"It would have been better so!" said Hester Prynne.

"What evil have I done the man?" asked Roger Chillingworth. "If I had not cared for him, his life would have burned away in torment within two years of the crime that you and he share. I have used all my skill to keep him alive. That he now breathes and walks about on earth is all due to me!"

"Better he had died at once!" Hester said.

"Yes, woman, that's all too true!" cried old Roger Chillingworth, letting the lurid fire of his heart blaze out before her eyes. "Better had he died at once! Never did mortal suffer what this man has suffered. And all in the sight of his worst enemy! He has felt an influence dwelling always upon him like a curse. But he knew not that it was my hand squeezing his heart. In his foolish superstition, he imagined himself given over to a fiend to torture him as a foretaste of what waits for him beyond the grave. But it was the constant shadow of my presence! I, the man he wronged! I, who has grown to exist only for this poison of dire revenge! Yes! There was a fiend at his elbow! A mortal man, who once had a human heart, has become a fiend for his special torment!"

The unfortunate physician lifted his hands with a look of horror, as if he beheld some unrecognizable and frightful shape that had taken the place of his own image in a mirror. He had never before viewed himself as he did now.

"Have you not tortured him enough?" said Hester, noticing the old man's look. "Has he not paid for his wrong to you?"

"No! He has only increased his debt!" answered the physician, subsiding into gloom. "Do you remember me, Hester, as I was nine years ago when we were last together in Amsterdam? Even then, I was in my autumn days, nor was it the early autumn. My life had been made up of studious, thoughtful, quiet years. My only desire was to increase my knowledge and, if possible, advance human welfare through my knowledge. No life had been more peaceful and innocent than mine. Do you remember me? Was I not a man thoughtful of others, craving little for myself—kind, true, just, and of constant, though not warm, affections? Was I not all this?"

"All this, and more," Hester said.

"And what am I now?" he demanded, looking into her face and permitting the whole evil within him to be written on his features. "I have already told you what I am—a fiend! Who made me so?"

"It was I," cried Hester, shuddering. "It was I, just as much as he. Why have you not taken revenge on me?"

"I have left you to the scarlet letter," replied Roger Chillingworth. "If that has not avenged me, I can do no more!"

He put his finger on the letter and smiled.

"It has avenged you!" answered Hester.

"As I thought it would," the physician said. "And now, what did you want to say to me about this man?"

"I must reveal the secret," Hester answered firmly. "He must know you in your true character. What will come of it, I know not. I will not beg that you show him mercy because I do not see any advantage to his living any longer a life of ghastly emptiness. Do with him as you will, but he must know who you are. There is no good for him—no good for me—no good for you! There is no good for little Pearl! There is no path to guide us out of this dismal maze."

"Woman, I could almost pity you!" said Roger Chillingworth, unable to restrain a thrill of admiration. "I pity you for the good that has been wasted on your nature."

"And I you," answered Hester Prynne, "for the hatred that has transformed a wise and just man into a fiend. Will you not purge it out and be once more human? Forgive and leave his punishment to heaven. I said there could be no good for any of us, wandering together in this gloomy maze of evil, stumbling over the guilt with which we have strewn our path. But it is not so. There might be good for you, and you alone, since you have been deeply wronged and have the power to forgive. Will you give up that privilege? Will you reject that priceless benefit?"

"Peace, Hester!" replied the old man with gloomy sternness. "It is not my place to forgive. I have no such power. By your first misstep, you did plant the germ of evil. But since that moment, all has been a dark necessity. You that wronged me are not sinful. Neither am I fiend-like that have snatched a fiend's work from his hands. It is our fate. Let the black flower blossom as it will. Now go your way and deal with him as you will."

He waved his hand and turned back to his task of gathering herbs.

CHAPTER 15

Hester and Pearl

So Roger Chillingworth—a deformed old figure, with a face that haunted men's memories longer than they liked—took leave of Hester Prynne and went stooping away along the earth. He gathered here and there an herb or grubbed up a root and put it into the basket on his arm. Hester gazed after him a little while. She half-imagined that she would see the tender grass of early spring be blighted beneath him. She wondered what sort of herbs he gathered. Did the earth, in response to his evil eye, greet him with poisonous shrubs? Or did his touch convert harmless plants into deadly compounds? Did the sun, which shone so brightly everywhere else, really fall upon him? Or was there, as it seemed, a circle of threatening shadow moving along with his deformed figure? Would he suddenly sink into the earth, leaving a barren and blasted spot where, in time, deadly nightshade would grow? Or would he spread bat's wings and flee away, looking so much uglier the higher he rose toward heaven?

"Whether it's a sin or not," said Hester bitterly as she gazed after him, "I hate the man!"

She thought of those long-past days, first in England then Amsterdam. He would emerge from his study in the evening, saying he needed to bask in her smile in order to take the chill of so many lonely hours with his books off his heart. As she looked back on such scenes now, they seemed among the ugliest of her remembrances. She marveled at how she could have ever allowed herself to be convinced to marry him. She judged it her worst crime that she had ever endured the lukewarm grasp of his hand and had permitted the smile of her lips and eyes to mingle and melt into his own. That he had persuaded her to imagine herself happy by his side seemed a worse offense than any he had suffered from her actions.

"Yes, I hate him!" repeated Hester, more bitterly than before. "He betrayed me! He has done worse wrong to me than I did to him!"

The emotions of that moment threw a dark light on Hester's state of mind. As she stood gazing after the crooked figure of old Roger

Chillingworth, her words revealed much that she might not otherwise have acknowledged to herself.

After he was gone, she called her child back.

"Pearl! Little Pearl! Where are you?"

Pearl had been at no loss for entertainment while her mother talked with the old herb-gatherer. For a while, she had continued to pursue her own image in a pool of water. She tried to beckon the phantom to come forth and, when it declined, she attempted to find a passage for herself into its sphere of existence.

Soon, however, she found that either she or the image was unreal and she turned to other entertainments. She made little boats of pieces of bark and set them asail. She seized a horseshoe crab by the tail and dragged it along the water's edge. She laid out a jellyfish to melt in the sun. Then she took up the white foam that streaked the line of the advancing tide. This she threw upon the breeze, then scampered after it to catch the great snowflakes before they fell. Noticing a flock of sea birds feeding along the shore, the naughty child filled her apron with pebbles and, creeping close to the birds, pelted them with her missiles. One little gray bird, Pearl was almost sure, had been hit and fluttered away with a broken wing. But then the elf-child sighed and gave up the game. It grieved her to have done harm to a little being that was as wild as the sea breeze, or as wild as Pearl herself.

Her final game was to gather seaweed of various kinds and make herself a scarf and a head-dress and make herself look like a little mermaid. As a last touch, she took some eelgrass and imitated as best she could the decoration with which she was so familiar on her mother's breast. A letter—the letter A—but freshly green instead of scarlet!

"I wonder if mother will ask me what it means!" thought Pearl, as she looked at her creation.

Just then she heard her mother's voice. Flitting along as lightly as one of the little sea birds, Pearl appeared before Hester, dancing, laughing, and pointing her finger to the ornament on her chest.

"My little Pearl," Hester said after a moment's silence, "the green letter on you has no significance. But do you know, my child, the meaning of this letter that I am doomed to wear?"

"Yes, Mother," the child said. "It is the great letter A. You have taught it to me in the reading book."

Hester looked steadily into her little face. She could not satisfy herself whether Pearl really attached any meaning to the symbol.

"Do you know, child, why your mother wears this letter?"

"Truly, I do!" Pearl answered, looking brightly into her mother's face. "It is for the same reason the minister keeps his hand over his heart!"

"And what reason is that?" asked Hester. "What does the letter have to do with any heart other than my own?"

"I have told you all I know, Mother," Pearl said, in a more serious tone than she usually used. "Ask the old man that you were just talking with. Maybe he can tell. But really, Mother, what does the letter mean? And why do you wear it? And why does the minister keep his hand over his heart?"

She took her mother's hand in both her own and gazed into her eyes with an earnestness that was seldom seen in her wild and fanciful character. The thought occurred to Hester that the child might be trying to establish a meeting point of sympathy. Hester loved the child dearly but, until now, had hoped for little in return. In the little chaos of Pearl's character, there might be seen emerging an unflinching courage, a sturdy pride, and a bitter scorn of things the child felt were tainted with falsehood. With all these fine attributes, thought Hester, this elfish child could grow into a noble woman, in spite of the evil she had inherited from her mother.

All her short life, Pearl's fascination with the mystery of the scarlet letter seemed an innate quality of her being. Hester had often thought it was part of her own punishment that Pearl was always intrigued by the symbol. But now, for the first time, Hester wondered if the child's fascination might also be a link to mercy and kindness. Might it not be the child's mission to soothe away the sorrow that lay cold in her mother's tomb-like heart? And possibly to help her overcome the wild passion that lay imprisoned within that heart?

Such were the thoughts that now stirred in Hester's mind. And there was little Pearl, all this while, holding her mother's hand in both her own. Turning her face upward, the child asked these searching questions once, and again, and still a third time.

"What does the letter mean, Mother? And why do you wear it? And why does the minister keep his hand over his heart?"

"What shall I say?" Hester thought to herself. "No. If this is the price of the child's sympathy, I cannot pay it!"

"Silly Pearl," she said, "what questions are these? There are many things in this world that a child must not ask about. What do I know of the minister's heart? And as for the scarlet letter, I wear it for the sake of its gold thread!"

In all the past seven years, Hester Prynne had never before been false to the symbol on her breast. It was as if, in spite of the strict watch that she kept over her heart, some new evil had crept in that made her answer as she did. As for little Pearl, the earnestness soon passed out of her face.

But the child did not see fit to let the matter drop. Two or three times as she and her mother went homeward, she asked again. And yet again at suppertime. That evening, while Hester was putting her to bed, Pearl looked up with mischief gleaming in her black eyes.

"Mother," she said, "what does the scarlet letter mean?"

And the next morning when the child awoke, she asked the other question which she had come to connect with her investigation of the topic—

"Mother! Mother! Why does the minister keep his hand over his heart?"

"Hold your tongue, naughty child!" answered Hester, with greater sharpness than she had ever used with the child. "Do not tease me or I will put you into a dark closet!"

CHAPTER 16

A Forest Walk

Hester Prynne remained steadfast in her decision to warn Mr. Dimmesdale of the true character of the physician who watched him so closely. For several days, she waited for an opportunity to speak with him while he was on one of his solitary walks in the wooded hills beyond the town. She chose not to visit him in his own study. She did not want any interference from old Roger Chillingworth. And she felt that both she and the minister would need the whole wide world to breathe in while they talked together.

At last she learned, while attending to a sick townsperson, that the Reverend Mr. Dimmesdale had gone the day before to visit John Eliot who was preaching among his Indian converts. He was expected to return at a particular hour in the afternoon of the next day. Therefore, the next day, Hester took little Pearl—as she always did—and set out.

After the two had crossed from the peninsula to the mainland, the road became no more than a footpath. It straggled onward into the mystery of the primeval forest. The trees stood black and dense on either side. They hemmed in the path so narrowly that the sky was hidden from view except for an occasional glimpse. To Hester's mind, the image was not unlike the moral wilderness in which she had so long been wandering.

The day was chilly and somber. Overhead was an expanse of gray cloud. Occasionally, this was stirred by a breeze, so that a gleam of flickering sunshine could now and then be seen at its solitary play along the path. This flitting cheerfulness was always at the farther extremity of some long vista through the forest. The playful sunlight withdrew itself as they came close. This left the places where it had danced that much drearier because they had hoped to find them bright.

"Mother," said little Pearl, "the sunshine does not love you. It runs away and hides because of the letter on your dress. There it is, playing a good way off. You stay here and let me run and catch it. I am just a child. It will not flee from me because I am not wearing a letter on my dress yet!"

"Nor ever will, my child, I hope," said Hester.

"And why not, Mother?" asked Pearl. "Will it not come of its own accord when I am a grown woman?"

"Run away, child," answered her mother, "and catch the sunshine! It will soon be gone."

Pearl raced off. Hester smiled to see that the child did actually catch the sunshine. She stood laughing in the midst of it, all brightened by its splendor and sparkling with liveliness. The light lingered about the lonely child, as if glad to have such a playmate. In a moment, her mother had drawn almost close enough to step into the magic circle too.

"It will go now!" said Pearl, shaking her head.

"Watch!" answered Hester, smiling. "I can stretch out my hand and grasp some of it."

As she attempted to do so, the sunshine vanished. Judging from the bright expression that was dancing on Pearl's face, her mother could have imagined that the child had absorbed it into herself. Perhaps the child would let it shine forth again as they plunged into some gloomier shade on the path. It was the sense of unbound energy in Pearl's spirit that always impressed Hester. She did not have the disease of sadness that so many children inherit from the troubles of their ancestors. She lacked a grief that deeply touched her and would humanize her and make her capable of sympathy. But there was time enough yet for little Pearl!

"Come, my child," Hester said. "We will sit down a little way from the path and rest ourselves."

"I am not tired, Mother," replied the little girl. "But you may sit down, if you will tell me a story while you rest."

"A story, child!" Hester said. "About what?"

"A story about the Black Man!" Pearl answered. She took hold of her mother's dress and looked up, half-earnestly, half-mischievously, into her face. "How he hunts this forest and carries a book with him—a big, heavy book with iron clasps. And how this ugly Black Man offers his book and an iron pen to everybody that meets him among the trees. And they are to write their names with their own blood. And then he sets his mark on each one's chest! Did you ever meet the Black Man, Mother?"

"And who told you this story, Pearl?" asked her mother, recognizing a common superstition of the period.

"It was the old woman sitting by the fireplace in the house where you tended the sick person last night," the child said. "She thought I was asleep while she talked of it. She said that thousands and thousands of people have met him here and written in his book and have his mark on them. She said the ugly-tempered old Mistress Hibbins was one of them. And, Mother, the old woman said that this scarlet letter was the Black Man's mark on you. She said it glows like a red flame when you meet him at midnight here in the dark wood. Is it true, Mother? And do you go to meet him in the nighttime?"

"Did you ever awake and find me gone?" asked Hester.

"Not that I remember," the child said. "If you fear leaving me in the cottage, you could take me with you. I would very gladly go! But, Mother, tell me. Is there such a Black Man? And did you ever meet him? And is this his mark?"

"If I tell you, will you let me have some peace?" asked her mother.

"Yes, if you tell me all," answered Pearl.

"Once in my life I met the Black Man!" said her mother. "This scarlet letter is his mark!"

As they talked, they had moved deep enough into the wood to keep from being observed by any casual passer-by along the path. They seated themselves on a luxuriant heap of moss—the remains of what had been a gigantic pine in the previous century. Close by flowed a brook, its leaf-strewn banks rising gently on either side. Here and there, the overhanging trees had flung down great branches which choked up the current, compelling it to form eddies and black depths. Elsewhere, it ran more swiftly and in these livelier passages appeared a channelway of pebbles and brown, sparkling sand.

Letting the eyes follow along the course of the stream, they could catch the reflected light from its water for a short distance into the forest. But soon it disappeared amid the bewilderment of tree trunks and underbrush and sometimes a huge rock, covered over with gray lichen. The giant trees and boulders of granite seemed intent on making a mystery of the course of the brook. It was as if they feared, with its never-ceasing babbling, it would whisper tales out of the heart of the old forest where it flowed. Continually, as it stole onward, the streamlet kept up a babble, kind, quiet, soothing, but melancholy—like the voice of a young child that was spending its infancy without playfulness and knew not how to be merry among sad acquaintances.

"Oh, foolish and tiresome little brook!" cried Pearl after listening a while to its talk. "Why are you so sad? Pluck up your spirit, and do not always be sighing and murmuring!"

But the brook, in the course of its little lifetime among the forest trees, had gone through so solemn an experience that it could not help talking about it. It seemed to have nothing else to say. Pearl resembled the brook in that the current of her life gushed from a source as mysterious and flowed through scenes shadowed as heavily with gloom. But, unlike the little stream, she danced and sparkled and chattered airily along her course.

"What does the sad little brook say, Mother?" she asked.

"If you had a sorrow of your own, the brook might tell you of it," answered Hester, "even as it is telling me of mine. But now, Pearl, I hear someone on the path. Go play and leave me to speak with he who comes."

"Is it the Black Man?" asked Pearl.

"Will you go and play, child?" repeated her mother. "But do not stray far into the wood. And come right back when I call."

"Yes, Mother," answered Pearl. "But, if it is the Black Man, will you not let me stay a moment and look at him?"

"Go, silly child!" said her mother impatiently. "It is not the Black Man! You can see him now through the trees—it is the minister!"

"So it is!" said the child. "And, Mother, he has his hand over his heart! Is it because, when the minister wrote his name in the book, the Black Man set his mark in that place? But why doesn't he wear it outside his clothing, as you do, Mother?"

"Go now, child, and you can tease me as you wish some other time!" cried Hester Prynne. "But do not go far. Do not go any farther than the sound of the brook."

The child went singing away, following up

the current of the brook, as if to make it less melancholy. But the little stream would not be comforted. It still kept telling its unintelligible secret of some mournful mystery that had happened—or was yet to happen—within the dismal forest. So Pearl, who had enough of shadow in her own little life, chose to break off all acquaintance with this complaining brook. She set to gathering violets and scarlet columbines that she found growing in the crevices of a rock.

When her elf-child had departed, Hester Prynne took a step or two toward the path, but still remained under the deep shadow of the trees. She saw the minister, entirely alone and leaning on a walking stick he had cut from beside the path. He looked haggard and feeble. He had an air of nervous sorrow, which always remained hidden when he walked in town. He moved listlessly, as if he saw no reason for taking one step further. He looked ready to throw himself down on the nearest tree root and lie there forever. The leaves might cover him, and the soil gradually accumulate over his body, no matter whether there was life in it or not. Death was too definite an object to be wished for or avoided.

To Hester's eye, the Reverend Mr. Dimmesdale showed no symptom of specific suffering, except that, as little Pearl had remarked, he kept his hand over his heart.

CHAPTER 17

The Pastor and His Parishioner

Even though the minister walked slowly, he had almost gone by before Hester Prynne could gather enough voice to attract his attention.

"Arthur Dimmesdale!" she said, faintly at first, then louder. "Arthur Dimmesdale!"

"Who speaks?" answered the minister.

Gathering himself up quickly, he stood straighter. He seemed like a man taken by surprise in a mood he did not want others to see. Looking anxiously in the direction of the voice, he indistinctly saw a form under the trees. Although it was noontime, the clouds and the heavy foliage made it difficult to tell if the darkly clothed figure was a woman or a shadow. It may be that his pathway through life was haunted in this way—by a specter that had stolen out from among his thoughts.

He moved a step closer and discovered the scarlet letter.

"Hester! Hester Prynne!" he said. "Is it you? Are you in life?"

"It is so!" she answered. "In such life as has been mine these past seven years. And you, Arthur Dimmesdale, do you yet live?"

It was no wonder that they so questioned one another's actual bodily existence and even doubted their own. This was a strange meeting in the dim wood. It was like a first meeting beyond the grave of two spirits that had been intimately connected in their former life. Now they stood coldly shuddering, in mutual dread—each a ghost, and awestruck at the other ghost! And they were awestruck at themselves, as well. The moment flung back to them their consciousness and revealed to each heart its history and experience. The soul beheld its features in the mirror of the passing moment. It was with fear and trembling that Arthur Dimmesdale put forth his hand, chill as death, and touched the chill hand of Hester Prynne. The grasp, cold as it was, took away the dreariest aspect of the meeting. They now felt themselves, at least, inhabitants of the same sphere.

Without a word more spoken, they glided back into the shadow of the woods and sat down on the heap of moss. When they were able to speak, it was at first only to utter remarks that any two acquaintances might have made—about the gloomy sky, the threatening storm, the health of each other. And so they moved, step by step, into thoughts that were brooding deepest in their hearts. They had been estranged so long by fate and circumstances that they needed something casual to start. These matters threw open the doors of conversation so that their real thoughts might be led across the threshold.

After a while, the minister fixed his eyes on Hester Prynne's.

"Hester," he said, "have you found peace?"

She smiled drearily, looking down at the scarlet letter.

"Have you?" she asked.

"None! Nothing but despair!" he answered. "What else could I expect, being what I am and leading such a life? All of God's gifts that were originally in me have become instruments of spiritual torment. Hester, I am miserable!"

"The people respect you," Hester said. "You do much good among them. Does this bring you no comfort?"

"Only the more misery, Hester" answered the clergyman, with a bitter smile. "I may appear to do good, but I have no faith in it. It is a delusion. What can a ruined soul like mine do to redeem the souls of others? I stand in the pulpit and see my flock listening to my words, believing them to be truth. Then I look inward and see the black reality of what they idolize. I have laughed in bitterness and agony of heart at the contrast between what I seem to be and what I am! And Satan laughs at it!"

"No, you are wrong," Hester said gently. "You have deeply and sorely repented. Your sin is left behind you long ago. Your present good works are no less holy than they seem to others. Shouldn't this bring you peace?"

"No, Hester!" replied the clergyman. "There is no substance in it. It is cold and dead and can do nothing for me. I should long ago have thrown off this clothing of mock holiness and have shown myself to mankind as they will see me on the Day of Judgment. You, Hester, wear the scarlet letter openly! Mine burns in secret! I have lived in torment for seven years! You little know what a relief it is to look into an eye that recognizes me for what I am! Had I but one friend—or even my worst enemy!—to whom I could unburden my heart daily when I grow sick of the praises of other men! Even that little bit of truth would save me and keep me alive. But now, all is falsehood! All is emptiness! All death!"

Hester Prynne looked into his face but hesitated to speak. Yet his very words did invite what she had come to tell him. She conquered her fears and spoke.

"Such a friend as you have just wished for, you have in me, the partner in your sin." She hesitated but brought the words out with an effort. "And you have long had such an enemy. You dwell with him under the same roof!"

The minister started to his feet, gasping for breath and clutching at his heart as if to tear it out of his breast.

"What are you saying?" he cried. "An enemy? And under my own roof? What do you mean?"

Hester Prynne now fully realized the depth of the injury she had caused by permitting the minister to remain at the mercy of the evil old man for so many years. Just having such a malevolent enemy so close was enough to disturb the magnetic sphere of a person as sensitive as Arthur Dimmesdale. Since seeing the minister the night of his vigil, all Hester's sympathies toward him had been softened and invigorated. She now read his heart more accurately. His constant exposure to the secret poison of Roger Chillingworth's presence had irritated his conscience and corrupted his spiritual being. Its result could hardly fail to be insanity and eternal alienation from the Good and True.

This was the ruin she had brought upon the man she still so passionately loved! Hester felt that the sacrifice of Dimmesdale's good name—or even his death—would have been preferable to the alternative which she had chosen that night in the prison with Chillingworth. And now, she would gladly have died rather than have to face this grievous wrong she had done.

"Oh, Arthur," she cried, "forgive me! In all things I have tried to be true. Truth was the one virtue I held fast—except when your good name was to be put into question. Then I consented to deception. But a lie is never good, even if death is the alternative. Do you not understand? That old man—the physician—the one called Roger Chillingworth—he was my husband!"

The minister looked at her for an instant with a violence of passion that sprang from the part of him that the Devil claimed. Never was there a blacker or fiercer frown than the one Hester now encountered. For the brief moment it lasted, it was a dark transformation. Then he sank down on the ground and buried his face in his hands.

"I might have known it!" he murmured. "I did know it! The secret was told to me by the way I felt my heart shrink back when I first met him. Why did I not understand? Oh, Hester Prynne, you little know all the horror of this thing! And the shame! The ugliness of the exposure of a guilty heart to the very eye that would take pleasure in it! Woman, you are accountable for this! I cannot forgive you!"

"You shall forgive me!" cried Hester, flinging herself on the fallen leaves beside him. "Let God punish! You shall forgive!"

With sudden, desperate tenderness, she threw her arms around him and pressed his head against her breast. She cared not that his cheek rested against the scarlet letter. He struggled to release himself. But Hester would not set him free, for fear he should look sternly in her face. For seven years, all the world had frowned at this lonely woman—and she bore it, never once turning away. And Heaven had frowned upon her—and she had not died. But the frown of this pale, weak, sinful, sorrow-stricken man was what Hester could not bear, and live!

"Will you forgive me?" she repeated over and over. "Will you not frown? Will you forgive?"

"I do forgive you, Hester," replied the minister with deep sadness. "I freely forgive you now. May God forgive us both! We are not, Hester, the worst sinners in the world. There is one worse than even the polluted priest! That old man's revenge has been blacker than my sin. He has violated, in cold blood, the sanctity of a human heart. You and I, Hester, never did so!"

"Never, never!" she whispered. "What we did had a consecration of its own. We felt it to be so! We said so to each other! Have you forgotten?"

"Hush, Hester," said Arthur Dimmesdale, rising from the ground. "No. I have not forgotten."

They sat down again, side by side, hand clasped in hand, on the mossy trunk of the fallen tree. Life had never brought them a gloomier hour. The forest was dark around them and creaked with a gust of wind that was passing through it. The boughs were tossing heavily above their heads. One solemn old tree groaned dolefully to another, as if telling the sad story of the pair that sat beneath, or warning of evil to come.

And yet they lingered. The forest path that led back to the settlement looked dreary. There Hester Prynne must take up again the burden of her shame. There Arthur Dimmesdale must take up again the hollow mockery of his good name. So they lingered an instant longer. No golden light had ever been so precious as the gloom of this dark forest. Here, seen only by his eyes, the scarlet letter need not burn into the breast of the fallen woman. Here, seen only by her eyes, Arthur Dimmesdale, false to God and man, might be, for one moment, true.

He started at a thought that suddenly occurred to him.

"Hester," he cried, "here is a new horror! Roger Chillingworth knows your intention to speak with me. Will he continue, then, to keep our secret? What direction will his revenge now take?"

"There is a strange secrecy in his nature," replied Hester, thoughtfully. "I think it unlikely that he will betray the secret. He will, no doubt, seek other means of satisfying his dark passion."

"And I! How am I to continue living while breathing the same air with this deadly enemy?" exclaimed Arthur Dimmesdale, shrinking within himself. "Think for me, Hester! You are strong.

Decide for me!"

"You must no longer dwell with this man," Hester said slowly and firmly. "Your heart must no longer be under his evil eye."

"But how can I avoid it?" the minister replied. "What other choice do I have? Should I lie down again on these withered leaves and die at once? Be strong for me. Advise me what to do!"

"Is the world so narrow?" exclaimed Hester, fixing her deep eyes on the minister's. "Does the whole universe lie within the boundaries of the town? You say the forest path leads back to the settlement. And it does. But it also leads away from town. Deeper it goes into the wilderness. Within a few miles, you will find no trace of the white man's footsteps. There you are free! So brief a journey would bring you to a world where you may still be happy. Is there not enough shade in all this boundless forest to hide your heart from the gaze of Roger Chillingworth?"

"Yes, Hester. But only in a grave under the fallen leaves!" replied the minister, with a sad smile.

"Then there is the broad pathway of the sea!" continued Hester. "It brought you here and it can take you back. You would be beyond his power and knowledge in a rural village or in London in England—or surely in Germany or France or pleasant Italy."

"It cannot be!" answered the minister. "I am powerless to go. Sinful as I am, I must continue my earthly existence in the sphere where Providence has placed me. Lost as my own soul is, I would still do what I can for other human souls!"

"You are crushed under the weight of seven years of misery," replied Hester, determined to buoy him up with her own energy. "Leave it all behind you! Start over, in the wilderness or across the sea. The future is full of promise and success. There is happiness to be enjoyed! There is good to be done! Exchange this false life of yours for a true one. Do anything, save lie down and die! Give up the name Arthur Dimmesdale and take a name you can wear without fear or shame. Why would you spend another day in this place that has gnawed into your life with torment? Go from here!"

"Oh, Hester!" cried Arthur Dimmesdale. A fitful light, kindled by her enthusiasm, flashed up in his eyes and died away. "You tell a man whose knees are tottering that he should run a race! I must die here. There is not the strength or courage left in me to venture into the strange, difficult world alone!"

It was the last expression of dejection of a broken spirit. He lacked the energy to grasp the better fortune that seemed within his reach.

He repeated the word.

"Alone, Hester!"

"You shall not go alone!" she answered, in a deep whisper.

Then, all was spoken.

CHAPTER 18

A Flood of Sunshine

Arthur Dimmesdale gazed into Hester's face with a look of hope and joy. But mixed with those emotions were fear and a kind of horror at her boldness. She had spoken what he had vaguely hinted at but dared not speak.

Hester Prynne's life over these past seven years had made her used to ways of thinking that were altogether foreign to the clergyman. She had wandered without guidance in moral wilderness. It was a place as vast and shadowy as the untamed forest where they now sat. She roamed as freely as the wild Indian in his woods. For years she had looked at society from an estranged position. This had set her free. The scarlet letter was her passport into regions where other women dared not tread.

The minister, on the other hand, had never

gone through an experience that led him beyond the range of generally accepted laws. Only once in his life had he overstepped the limits of one of those laws. But that had been a sin of passion, not a purposeful or willful transgression. Ever since that moment, he had carefully watched every breath of emotion and every thought. He vigorously guarded against any further misstep. His sin had made him more driven to live safely within society's laws than if he had never sinned at all.

In this respect, the whole seven years of isolation and humiliation had prepared Hester for this very moment. But Arthur Dimmesdale! Were such a man to fall once more, what excuse could there be for his crime? None—unless that he had been broken down by his long and painful private suffering. In truth, the break that sin makes in the wall of the human soul can never be fully repaired in this life. It may be watched and guarded. But there is still the ruined wall. And near it is the stealthy footstep of the foe that would again rush through that break.

The clergyman resolved to flee, and not alone.

"If, in all these past seven years," he thought, "I could recall one instant of peace or hope, I would continue in my present life for the sake of Heaven's mercy. But, since I am irrevocably doomed, why should I not take this chance? I cannot live any longer without her companionship. Her power sustains me, her tenderness soothes me."

"You will go," said Hester calmly, as he met her glance.

The decision made, a glow of strange enjoyment threw its flickering brightness over his troubled soul. He felt like a prisoner just escaped from the dungeon of his own heart. It was the thrilling effect of breathing the wild, free atmosphere of an unchristianized, lawless region. His spirit rose.

"Do I feel joy again?" he cried, wondering at himself. "I had thought the spark of it was dead in me! Hester, you are my better angel! I have risen up anew, with better powers to glorify Him that has shown me mercy! This is already a better life! Why did we not find it sooner?"

"We should not look back," answered Hester. "The past is gone. Why linger there now? See! With this symbol I will undo it all, and make it as if it had never been!"

As she spoke, she undid the clasp that fastened the scarlet letter. Taking it from her breast, she threw it a distance among the withered leaves. The mystic token alighted on the near edge of the stream. A little further, and it would have fallen into the water, giving the little brook another tale of sorrow to murmur about. But there lay the embroidered letter, glittering like a lost jewel but haunted by strange phantoms of guilt.

The stigma gone, Hester heaved a long, deep sigh. She felt the burden of shame and anguish depart from her spirit. By another impulse, she took off the formal cap that confined her hair. Down it fell upon her shoulders, dark and rich. It imparted a charm of softness on her features. A radiant and tender smile played around her mouth and beamed from her dark eyes. Her cheek—so long pale—was glowing with a crimson flush. The whole richness of her beauty and her youth flowed back into her within the magic circle of this hour. As if responding to these two mortal hearts, the gloom of the earth and sky vanished with their sorrow. All at once, as with a sudden smile from heaven, the sunshine burst forth, pouring a very flood of light into the obscure forest. The formerly shadowy objects embodied brightness now. The course of the little brook could now be traced by its merry gleam far into the wood's heart of mystery. And that heart of mystery had become a mystery of joy.

Such was the sympathy of Nature with the joy of these two human spirits.

Hester looked at Dimmesdale with the excitement of another joy.

"You must know Pearl!" she said. "Our little Pearl! I know you have seen her, but now you will see her with other eyes. She is a strange child. I hardly understand her. But you will love her dearly, as I do. And you will help me know how to deal with her."

"Do you think the child will be glad to know me?" asked the minister uneasily. "I have never been comfortable with children because they seem reluctant to be familiar with me. I have even been afraid of little Pearl."

"Oh, that is sad!" answered the mother. "But she will love you dearly, and you her. She is close by. I will call her."

Arthur Dimmesdale saw the child standing in a streak of sunshine, a good distance away, on the other side of the brook. "So you think the child will love me?" he asked.

Hester smiled and called to Pearl. She looked like a brightly-dressed vision in the sunbeam that fell upon her. The ray of light quivered to and fro, making her figure dim or distinct—now like a real child, now like a child's spirit. She heard her mother's voice and approached slowly through the forest.

Pearl had not been bored while her mother had been talking with the clergyman. The great black forest became the playmate of the lonely child. Somber as it was, it put on the kindest of its moods to welcome her. It offered her partridge berries. These Pearl gathered, and was pleased with their wild flavor. The small creatures of the woods hardly bothered to move out of her way. A dove, alone on a low branch, allowed Pearl to come close and uttered a sound as much of greeting as alarm. A fox was startled from his sleep by her light footsteps on the leaves. He looked questioningly at Pearl, as if wondering whether to steal off or renew his nap in the same spot. It is said—but this is surely improbable—that a wolf came up and sniffed at Pearl's dress and then offered his savage head to be patted by her hand. The truth seems to be that the mother forest and the wild creatures in it all recognized a kindred wildness in the human child.

And she was gentler here than in the streets of the settlement or in her mother's cottage. The flowers appeared to know it. As she passed, they seemed to whisper, "Decorate yourself with me, beautiful child! Decorate yourself with me!" And to please them, Pearl gathered violets and columbines and some twigs of the freshest green. With these she decorated her hair and her waist—and became a nymph child, a woodland fairy. In such a way was Pearl decorated when she heard her mother's voice and came slowly back.

Slowly, for she saw the clergyman.

CHAPTER 19

The Child at Brookside

"You will love her dearly," repeated Hester Prynne, as she and the minister sat watching little Pearl. "Is she not beautiful? Look at the natural skill with which she has decorated herself with those simple flowers. Diamonds and rubies would not be more becoming to her. She is a splendid child! I know whose eyes she has!"

"Do you know, Hester," said Arthur Dimmesdale, with an uneasy smile, "that this dear child has often caused me alarm. I thought that my own features were partly repeated in her face so clearly that the world would see them! But she looks more like you."

"No, no!" answered Hester, with a tender smile. "Soon you will not need to fear that she looks like you. She looks so strangely beautiful with those flowers in her hair. It is as if some woodland fairy had decorated her to meet us."

As they watched Pearl's slow advance, they felt as they had never felt before. In her was visible the tie that united them. For the past seven years, she had offered the world the living, mysterious symbol, which revealed the secret they so darkly sought to hide. The world lacked only the magician skilled enough to read the symbol. Pearl was the oneness of their being. How could they doubt that their earthly lives and future destinies were joined when they saw this material union and spiritual idea in little Pearl? Hester and Arthur's thoughts like these cast a magical spell about the child as she came onward.

"Do not let her see any unusual emotion as she approaches," whispered Hester. "Our Pearl is a fitful and fantastic elf sometimes. She rarely tolerates strong emotions when she does not fully comprehend the reason for them. But she has strong affections. She loves me, and she will love you!"

"You cannot imagine," the minister said, "how my heart dreads this meeting, yet yearns for it. As I told you, children do not warm to me. They stand apart and eye me strangely. Even little babies, when I take them in my arms, weep bitterly. But, twice in her lifetime, Pearl has been kind to me. The first time—you know it well—was when she looked up at me from the scaffold seven years ago. The second was when we met at the house of the governor."

"And you spoke so strongly on her behalf and mine," the mother answered. "I remember it, and so will little Pearl. Fear nothing! She may be strange and shy at first, but she will soon learn to love you!"

By this time Pearl had reached the edge of the brook. She stood on the far side, gazing silently at Hester and the clergyman, who still sat on the mossy tree-trunk. Just where she had paused, the brook formed a smooth and quite pool. This pool reflected a perfect image of her little figure. This image, so nearly identical with the living Pearl, seemed to communicate a shadowy and intangible quality to the child. It was strange the way the child stood, glorified in a ray of sunshine, looking at them though the forest gloom. In the brook beneath stood another child—another and the same—with its ray of golden light.

Hester felt herself in some manner estranged from Pearl. It was as if the child, in her lonely ramble through the forest, had strayed out of the sphere in which she and her mother had dwelt together. She seemed to be trying in vain to return to that sphere.

It is true that they were now estranged, but the fault was Hester's, not Pearl's. Since the child had rambled from her side, another person had been admitted within the circle of her mother's feelings. This had so changed the atmosphere that Pearl could not find her usual place and hardly knew where she was.

"I have the strange feeling," observed the minister, "that this brook is the boundary between two worlds and that you can never meet your Pearl again. Tell her to hurry. This delay makes me fearful."

"Come, dear child!" said Hester encouragingly, and stretching out both her arms. "How slow you are being! Here is a friend of mine who will be your friend as well. You will have twice as much love as before! Leap across the brook and come to us."

Pearl remained on the other side of the brook. She fixed her bright, wild eyes on her mother and the minister, as if to discover the relationship between them. For some unaccountable reason, as Arthur Dimmesdale felt the child's eyes upon him, his hand stole over his heart. At length Pearl stretched out her hand, with her index finger extended, pointed apparently toward her mother's breast. And beneath, in the mirror of the brook, there was the sunny image of Pearl, decorated with flowers, pointing her finger, too.

"Strange child, why do you not come to me?" exclaimed Hester.

Pearl continued to point and a frown gathered on her brow. As the mother kept beckoning to her and smiling, the child stamped her foot with yet a more imperious look and gesture. In the brook, again, was the fantastic beauty of the image, with its reflected frown, its pointing finger and imperious gesture.

"Hurry, Pearl, or I will be angry with you!" cried Hester Prynne. "Leap across the brook, naughty child, and run here! Otherwise, I will have to come get you!"

But Pearl was not at all startled by her mother's threats. She suddenly burst into a fit of passion, gesticulating violently and shrieking. The woods reverberated with her piercing cries on all sides. It seemed as if a hidden multitude were lending the lonely child their sympathy and encouragement. And seen in the brook was the shadowy wrath of Pearl's image, stamping its foot and wildly gesticulating—and still pointing its finger at Hester's breast!

In spite of a strong effort to conceal her trouble and annoyance, Hester turned pale. "I see what ails the child," she whispered to the clergyman. "Children will not accept the slightest change from the way things normally appear. Pearl misses something that she has always seen me wear."

"If you have a way to calm her," answered the minister, "do so immediately. I do not wish to encounter this passion in a child any more than I would want to face the wrath of an old witch, like Mistress Hibbins," he added with a smile. "In Pearl's young beauty, such emotion has an unearthly effect. Calm her, if you love me!"

"Pearl," said Hester, sadly, "Look down in front of you. There—on this side of the brook."

The child turned her eyes where Hester directed. There lay the scarlet letter, so close to the edge of the brook that the gold embroidery was reflected in it.

"Bring it here," Hester said.

"You come and pick it up!" answered Pearl.

"Was there ever such a child!" observed Hester aside to the minister. "But, in truth, she is right about this hateful token. I must bear its torture a few days longer—until we have left this region. The forest cannot hide it. But the mid-ocean shall swallow it up forever!"

With these words, she advanced to the edge of the brook, took up the scarlet letter, and fastened it again on her dress. But a moment ago Hester had hopefully spoken of drowning it in the deep sea. Now there was a sense of inevitable doom upon her as she received back this deadly symbol from the hand of fate. She had flung it into infinite space—she had drawn an hour's free breath—and here again was the scarlet misery, glittering in the old spot.

Hester next gathered up her long, flowing hair and confined it beneath her cap. As if there were a writhing spell in the sad letter, her beauty, the warmth and richness of her womanhood, departed, like fading sunshine. A gray shadow seemed to fall across her.

When the dreary change was complete, she extended her hand to Pearl.

"Do you know your mother now, child?" she asked. "Will you come across the brook to your mother, now that she has her shame upon her—now that she is sad?"

"Yes, now I will!" answered the child, bounding across the brook and clasping Hester in her arms. "Now you are my mother indeed! And I am your little Pearl!"

Pearl drew down her mother's head and kissed her on the cheek. Then she kissed the scarlet letter, too.

"That was not kind!" said Hester. "You show me a little love and then you mock me!"

"Why does the minister sit over there?" asked Pearl.

"He waits to welcome you," replied her mother. "Come and ask his blessing. He loves you, my little Pearl, and he loves your mother, too. Come. He wants to greet you."

"Does he love us?" said Pearl. "Will he go back with us, hand in hand, we three together, into town?"

"Not now, dear child," answered Hester. "But in days to come, he will walk hand in hand with us. We will have a home and fireside of our own. He will teach you many things and love you dearly. You will love him, will you not?"

"And will he always keep his hand over his

heart?" asked Pearl.

"Foolish child! What a question!" exclaimed her mother. "Come and ask his blessing."

But, whether from jealousy of a dangerous rival or from a whim of her freakish nature, Pearl would not show favor to the clergyman. It was only by leading Pearl by the hand that Hester brought her up to him. Even so, she hung back and made mischievous, imp-like faces.

The minister, painfully embarrassed, hoped that a kiss might prove the charm to win her over. He bent forward and touched his lips to her brow.

Immediately, Pearl broke away from her mother. Running to the brook, she stooped over and bathed her forehead until the unwelcome kiss was quite washed off. She then stood by the edge of the brook, silently watching Hester and the clergyman. They, meanwhile, talked together and made plans for how they should arrange their departure into a new life.

And now this fateful conversation had come to a close. The little valley was to be left in solitude among its dark, old trees with their multitudinous tongues. These would whisper long of what had passed there. And the melancholy brook would add this other tale to the mystery with which its little heart was already overburdened. It would continue its murmuring babble with no more cheerfulness of tone then in the ages past.

CHAPTER 20

The Minister in a Maze

As the minister departed, he threw a backward glance toward Hester Prynne and little Pearl. He half expected he would discover only some faint outline of the mother and the child, slowly fading into the twilight of the woods. But there was Hester, clad in her gray robe, still standing beside the moss-covered stump where they had sat together. And there was Pearl, dancing from the edge of the brook and taking her old place by her mother's side, now that the intrusive third person was gone. So the minister had not fallen asleep and dreamed!

As he continued along the path, he reviewed the plans that Hester and he had discussed for their departure. They had decided that the Old World with its crowds and cities offered the best shelter for them. Given the minister's talents and the state of his health, this seemed more promising than the American wilderness or one of the few European settlements scattered thinly along its seaboard.

It happened that there was a ship in Boston harbor at this time. It was one of those questionable cruisers that roamed the seas in those days. Such ships, although not absolutely outlaws of the deep, showed remarkable irresponsibility of character. This vessel had recently arrived from the Spanish Main. It would soon sail for England. Hester, through her self-appointed work as a Sister of Charity, had gotten to know the captain and crew. She would be able to secure passage secretly for two individuals and a child.

The minister had asked Hester when the vessel was expected to depart. It would probably set sail four days from now. "This is most fortunate!" he had said to himself. Three days from now, he was to preach the Election Sermon. This was a great honor, and he could think of no better way to end his professional career in New England. "At least they will say that I left no duty unperformed or ill performed!" he thought. Little did he know how he was deceiving himself. No man can for long wear one face to himself and another to the world without finally getting bewildered as to which may be true.

The excitement of Mr. Dimmesdale's feelings

gave him unusual physical energy. He hurried toward town at a rapid pace. The path among the woods seemed wilder than he had remembered it on his journey away from town two days earlier. He recalled how feebly he had moved and how he needed to pause frequently to catch his breath. Now, however, he leaped across muddy places and energetically climbed the hills and plunged into the hollows. The change astonished him.

As he got closer to town, he was struck by how different the familiar objects now looked to him. It seemed as if it were many days, or even years, since he last saw them. Even his own church seemed changed as he passed it. The front had a very strange, yet so familiar, appearance. It made Mr. Dimmesdale's mind vibrate between two ideas: either he had seen it only in a dream before today, or he was merely dreaming about it now.

The minister's own will, and Hester's will, had brought about this transformation. It was the same town as before. But the same minister had not returned from the forest. He might have said to friends who greeted him, "I am not the man you take me for! I left him in the forest, by a mossy tree-trunk, near a melancholy brook! Go look for your minister, and you will see his thin, pale figure flung down there like a cast-off cloak!"

Truly, he was a totally changed man. At every step he was tempted to do some strange, wild, wicked thing. For instance, he met one of his own deacons. The good old man, much admired for his work in the church, spoke to Mr. Dimmesdale with almost worshipping respect. During their brief conversation, it was only by the most careful self-control that Mr. Dimmesdale could keep himself from uttering certain blasphemous suggestions which came into his mind concerning Holy Communion. He absolutely trembled and turned pale as ashes for fear his tongue would utter these horrible matters. But even with this terror in his heart, he could hardly avoid laughing to imagine how the saintly old deacon would have been petrified by his minister's impiety!

Hurrying along the street, the Reverend Mr. Dimmesdale then encountered the oldest female member of his church. She was a poor and lonely widow with a heart of reminiscences about her dead husband and her dead children and her dead friends of long ago. But this devout soul took comfort in knowing that those who were gone were now in immortality with the Heavenly Father. One of her greatest earthly comforts was to meet her pastor and be refreshed with a word of warm, fragrant, heaven-breathing Gospel truth from his beloved lips into her ear. But on this occasion, up to the moment of putting his lips to the old woman's ear, Mr. Dimmesdale could recall no text of Scripture except a brief, unanswerable argument against the immortality of the human soul. Whispering such words to the old woman would probably have caused her to drop down dead at once, as if she were poisoned. Later, the minister could not recall what he really did whisper. Perhaps the old widow did not hear him distinctly or did not understand his message. Mr. Dimmesdale was reassured as he looked back to see an expression of divine gratitude that seemed like the shine of the celestial city on her wrinkled and ashy face.

After parting from the old parishioner, he met a younger member of his flock. She was a maiden newly won by his own sermon the Sabbath after his vigil on the scaffold. She was fair and pure as a lily that had bloomed in Paradise. The minister knew that she held him in the stainless sanctity of her heart, giving religion the warmth of love and giving love a religious purity. That afternoon, Satan must have led the poor young girl into the path of this lost and desperate man. As she approached, the arch-fiend whispered to Dimmesdale to drop into her tender breast a germ of evil that would blossom darkly and bear black fruit before long. Such was his sense of power over her virgin soul that the minister felt the strength to blight her whole field of innocence with but one wicked look. Struggling against this impulse, he held his cloak before his face and hurried by, showing no sign of recognition. Shocked, the girl spent hours attempting to figure out what fault in herself had caused the minister to ignore her.

Before the minister had time to celebrate his victory over this last temptation, he was possessed by an even more horrible impulse. He wanted to stop in the road and teach some very wicked words to a group of little Puritan children who were playing there. By again exerting great self-control, he was able to pass by without doing so.

"What haunts and tempts me this way?" he said to himself, pausing in the street and striking his hand against his forehead. "Am I mad? Did I make a contract with the Black Man in the forest?"

Just as he was having these thoughts, it is said that old Mistress Hibbins was passing by. Whether the witch had read the minister's thoughts or not, she stopped. Looking shrewdly into his face, she began a conversation.

"So, Reverend sir, you have made a visit into the forest," observed the witch lady, nodding her head. "The next time, let me know, and I will be pleased to keep you company. My good word will help you get a warm welcome from the great power that rules there."

"I must confess, madam," answered the clergyman, "that I am utterly bewildered as to what you mean. I did not meet any great power in the forest nor do I intend to. My journey to visit my godly friend John Eliot took me there. Nothing more."

"Ha, ha, ha!" cackled the old witch lady, still nodding. "Well, yes, we have to talk like that in the daytime! You carry it off like an old hand! But at midnight, and in the forest, we shall have other talk together!"

She passed on, often turning her head back and smiling at him.

"Have I in fact sold myself," thought the minister, "to the fiend whom the old hag has chosen as her prince and master?"

The minister had made a bargain very much like that. Tempted by a dream of happiness, he had given in to what he knew was deadly sin. And the infectious poison of that sin had rapidly spread through his moral system. Scorn, bitterness, ridicule of whatever was good and holy—all awoke to tempt and frighten him.

He had by this time reached his dwelling, next to the burial ground. Hurrying up the stairs, he took shelter in his study. He entered the familiar room and looked around at the books, the windows, the fireplace. He saw it with the same strangeness that had haunted his vision throughout his walk back to town. Here he had studied and written, gone through fast and vigil, tried to pray. There was the Bible. There on the table was the unfinished Election Sermon. He had stopped writing mid-sentence, when his thoughts had ceased to flow out onto the page two days before. He seemed to now stand apart and eye his former self with scornful, pitying curiosity. That self was gone! Another man had returned out of the forest, a wiser one, with a knowledge of hidden mysteries. A bitter kind of knowledge!

While lost in these thoughts, a knock came at the door. The minister said, "Come in!"—vaguely feeling that he might behold an evil spirit. And so he did! Old Roger Chillingworth entered. The minister stood, white and speechless, one hand on the Bible and the other on his chest.

"Welcome home, Reverend sir!" said the physician. "And how was that godly man, John Eliot? But, dear sir, you look pale. The journey has tired you. Will you not need my aid to strengthen you to preach the Election Sermon?"

"No, I do not think so, kind friend," answered the Reverend Dimmesdale. "My journey and the fresh air have done me good, after so long a confinement in my study. I believe I need no more of your drugs, my kind physician, even though they are good."

Although Roger Chillingworth gave no sign, the minister was almost convinced that the old man knew of the conversation with Hester that had just taken place. From the minister's point of view, then, the physician knew that he was no longer a trusted friend, but his bitterest enemy.

The physician, in his dark way, did creep frightfully close to the secret. "Would it not be better," he said, "to use my poor skill tonight? We must work to make you strong and vigorous for the Election Sermon. The people look for great things from you, sensing that, another year, they may find their pastor gone."

"Yes, gone to another world," replied the minister, with pious resignation. "In truth I do not expect to remain in this world through the flitting seasons of another year! But, kind sir, in my present condition, I have no need of your medicine."

"I am glad to hear it," answered the physician. "It may be that my remedies have begun to take effect. None would be happier than I if I could cause this cure."

"I thank you from my heart, my watchful friend," said the Reverend Mr. Dimmesdale, with a solemn smile. "I thank you and can only repay your good deeds with my prayers."

"A good man's prayers are better repayment than gold!" answered old Roger Chillingworth as he left the room.

Left alone, the minister summoned a servant to bring him food. He ate with ravenous appetite. Then, flinging the already written pages of the Election Sermon into the fire, he began to write another. He wrote with such an impulsive flow of thought and emotion that he felt as if he were inspired by Heaven. The night sped by. Morning came. The sunrise threw a golden beam into the study and across the minister's bedazzled eyes. There he was, with the pen still between his fingers, and a vast, immeasurable tract of written space behind him!

CHAPTER 21

The New England Holiday

Early in the morning of the day on which the new governor was to take office, Hester Prynne and little Pearl came into the marketplace. It was already filled with the craftsmen and other inhabitants of Boston, as well as with many people from the forest settlements that surrounded the town.

On this public holiday, as on every other day for the past seven years, Hester was dressed in coarse gray cloth. It had the effect of making her fade personally out of sight. At the same time, the scarlet letter brought her back from this twilight of indistinctness and revealed her under the moral aspect of its illumination. Her face had the frozen calmness of a dead woman's features.

But it might be that, today, there was an

imperceptible expression. After living under the gaze of the townspeople for seven miserable years, she now, for one last time, faced that gaze freely and voluntarily—as if to convert what had so long been an agony into a kind of triumph. "Look your last on the scarlet letter and its wearer!" one might imagine her saying. "In a little while, she will be beyond your reach! A few hours longer and the deep, mysterious ocean will hide forever the symbol you have caused to burn upon her breast!"

Pearl was gaily dressed in her usual manner. She contrasted so greatly with Hester that it would have been impossible to guess that this bright and sunny spirit owed its existence to the shape of gloomy gray. Her dress was as fitting to her as is the many-hued brilliance of a butterfly's wing is to that creature. On this day there was great excitement in her mood. She resembled the shimmer of a diamond with its sparkles and flashes. Pearl betrayed, by the very dance of her spirits, the emotions which none could detect in the marble passiveness of Hester's face.

Little Pearl flitted with a bird-like movement, rather than walking by her mother's side. She broke continually into shouts of wild, inarticulate music. When they reached the marketplace, she became still more restless.

"Why have people left their work today?" she asked. "Is it a playday for the whole world? See—

there is the blacksmith. And there is Master Brackett, the old jailer, nodding and smiling at me. Why is he doing that, Mother?"

"He remembers you as a little baby, my child," answered Hester.

"He should not smile so at me—the grimy, ugly-eyed old man!" said Pearl. "But look, Mother! There are so many faces of strange people, and Indians among them, and sailors! Why have they all come to the marketplace?"

"They are waiting to see the procession pass," Hester said. "The governor, the magistrates, and all the great people are to go by, with music and the soldiers marching before them."

"And will the minister be there?" asked Pearl. "And will he hold out his hands to me, as he did by the brook?"

"He will be there, child," answered her mother. "But he will not greet you today. Nor must you greet him."

"What a strange, sad man he is!" said the child, as if speaking partly to herself. "In the dark nighttime, he calls us to him and holds my hand while we all stand on the scaffold. And in the deep forest, where only the old trees can hear, he talks with you. And he kisses my forehead, too, so that the little brook would hardly wash it off. But here in the sunny day and among all the people, he knows us not! Nor must we know him! A strange, sad man he is, with his hand always over his heart!"

"Be quiet, Pearl! You do not understand these things," said her mother. "Do not think of the minister. Look around and see all the cheery faces! Today, a new man will begin to rule the people. They make merry and rejoice, as is the custom on this occasion."

It was as Hester said. Election Day was the one day on which Puritans celebrated in happiness and public joy. Such celebration was reminiscent of the pageantry their fathers had known in Elizabethan England. The procession before the people gave a needed dignity to the simple framework of a government so newly constructed.

The picture of human life in the marketplace, although dominated by the sad gray, brown, or black of the Puritan clothing, was made more lively by some diversity. A party of Indians stood close by, watching. They were dressed in their finery of curiously embroidered deerskin robes, wampum belts, red and yellow paint, and feathers. There were also several sailors from the vessel now in the harbor. They were rough-looking desperados with sun-blackened faces and great beards. From beneath their broad-brimmed hats gleamed eyes which, even in good nature and merriment, had a kind of animal ferocity. They casually broke the rules of behavior that were binding on all others. They smoked right under the beadle's nose. And they drank wine and rum from pocket-flasks and freely offered it to the gaping crowd around them.

The sea, in those days, heaved, swelled, and foamed very much at its own will, with hardly any attempts at regulation by human law. But a sailor might give up his nautical life at any time and turn to a respectable and pious life on land. Therefore, the Puritan elders smiled tolerantly at the rudeness of these seafarers. And there was not surprise in seeing so a reputable citizen as old Roger Chillingworth enter the marketplace in conversation with the commander of the questionable ship.

The commander was a showy and gallant figure. He wore colorful ribbons on his coat. His hat was decorated with gold lace, encircled by a gold chain, and topped with a feather. There was a sword at his side and a sword-cut on his forehead.

After parting from the physician, the commander strolled casually through the marketplace. In a few moments, he came upon Hester. She stood in a small, vacant area—a sort of magic circle. It was as if the crowd, though elbowing one another as they milled about, dared not to intrude on this space. The ship's commander, however, had no such qualms.

"So, mistress," said the captain, "I must tell the steward to prepare one more berth than you had requested! We'll have no fear of sickness on this voyage. What with the ship's surgeon and this other doctor, we need only fear too much medicine!"

"What do you mean?" asked Hester, more startled than she let show. "Do you have another passenger?"

"You did not know?" cried the shipmaster. "The physician—the one who calls himself Roger Chillingworth—will join you. You must have known it. He tells me he is with your party and a close friend of the gentleman you spoke to me about—the gentleman who is in danger from these sour old Puritan rulers!"

"Indeed, they know each other well," replied Hester, trying to appear calm despite what she was feeling. "They have long lived in the same house."

The shipmaster nodded and moved on. At that instant, Hester saw old Roger Chillingworth standing in the far corner of the marketplace and smiling at her. In spite of the distance and all the talk and laughter in the bustling square, it was a smile, which conveyed secret and fearful meaning.

CHAPTER 22

The Procession

Before Hester Prynne could gather her thoughts and decide how to handle this startling development, the sound of military music was heard approaching. It signaled the approach of the procession of magistrates and citizens on its way to the meetinghouse. That was where the Reverend Mr. Dimmesdale was to deliver the Election Sermon.

Soon the head of the procession appeared. In a slow and stately march, the procession turned a corner and made its way across the marketplace. First came the music. This gave a higher and more heroic air to the scene. For a moment, little Pearl was silent, lost in the music. She seemed to be borne upward, like a floating sea bird on the swelling sound. Then she quickly returned to her restless activity, brought back by the shimmer of sunshine on the weapons and bright armor of the military company that came next.

Next followed government officials of the colony. They were men who appear to have been chosen for their ponderous sobriety and seriousness, rather than brilliant intellect. After these magistrates came the young minister who was to deliver the Election Sermon. In those days, it was the men who chose this profession who had the intellectual ability, rather than those who chose the political life.

It seemed to those watching the procession that Mr. Dimmesdale showed greater energy now than at any moment since he first set foot on the New England shore. There was no feebleness of step. His body was not bent. His hand did not rest ominously over his heart. But the strength seemed not physical but spiritual, as if given to him by some angel. As his body moved forward with unusual force, it seemed as if he saw and heard nothing of what was around him. The spiritual element took up the feeble frame and carried it along.

Hester Prynne gazed steadily at the clergyman. As he approached, she felt a dreary influence come over her. He seemed so remote from her own sphere, and completely beyond her reach. She had imagined that, at this moment, one glance of recognition would pass between them. She thought of the dim forest with its valley of solitude and love and anguish. She thought of the mossy tree-trunk where, sitting hand in hand, they had mingled their sad and passionate talk with the melancholy murmur of the brook. How deeply they had known each other then! Was this the same man? She hardly knew him now! He, moving proudly past, enveloped, as it were, in the rich music, with the procession of majestic and honorable fathers.

Her spirit sank with the idea that all must have been a delusion. As vividly as she had dreamed it at the time, there could be no real bond between the clergyman and herself. She could scarcely forgive him—especially as their Fate approached—for being able so completely to withdraw himself from their mutual world, while she groped darkly and stretched forth her cold hands—and found him not.

Pearl either saw and responded to her mother's feelings, or herself felt the remoteness that had fallen around the minister. While the procession passed, the child was uneasy, fluttering up and down like a bird on the point of taking flight. When it had gone by, she looked up into Hester's face.

"Mother," she said, "was that the same minister that kissed me by the brook?"

"Hush, dear little Pearl!" whispered her mother. "We must not talk in the marketplace of what happens in the forest."

"I could not be sure it was the same man. He

looked so strange," continued the child. "Otherwise, I would have run to him. I would have asked him to kiss me, in front of all the people, as he did among the dark old trees. What would the minister have said, Mother? Would he have put his hand over his heart and scowled and told me to be gone?"

"What should he say, Pearl," answered Hester, "except that it was no time to kiss and that kisses are not given in the marketplace? It is lucky for you, foolish child, that you did not speak to him."

At that moment, Mistress Hibbins approached Hester. The old woman's eccentricities—or insanity—led her to do something few other townspeople would have dared: begin a conversation in public with the wearer of the scarlet letter. She was magnificently dressed in a gown of rich velvet and carried a gold-headed cane. Because of her reputation as one involved with black magic, the crowd gave way before her. They seemed to fear the touch of her dress, as if it carried the plague in its gorgeous folds.

"What mortal imagination could dream it!" whispered the old lady to Hester. "That saint on earth, as people see him. Who, seeing him now, would imagine how recently he left his study for a journey in the forest! We know what that means, Hester Prynne! I saw many a church member in the procession who has danced as I have when the Black Man in the forest was the fiddler. But this minister! Could you say for certain, Hester, whether this was the same man you encountered on the forest path?"

"Madam, I do not know what you are talking about," answer Hester. She was sure the old woman was not of sound mind. But even so, she was startled by the confidence with which Mistress Hibbins spoke of a personal connection between so many people and the Evil One. "It is not for me to talk lightly of a pious minister like the Reverend Mr. Dimmesdale."

"Fie, woman!" cried the old lady, shaking her finger at Hester. "Do you think I have been to the forest so many times and still have no skill to judge who else has been there? I know you, Hester, for anyone can see the token you wear. It glows like a red flame in the dark. You wear it openly. But this minister! Let me tell you! When the Black Man sees one of his own servants be so shy of acknowledging the bond, he is not pleased. He has a way of arranging things so that the mark will be revealed to the eyes of all the world! What does the Reverend Mr. Dimmesdale seek to hide with his hand always over his heart?"

"What is it, good Mistress Hibbins?" asked little Pearl eagerly. "Have you seen it?"

"No matter, darling!" responded Mistress Hibbins, looking closely at Pearl. "You yourself will see it one time or another. They say, child, that you are descended from the Prince of Air! Will you ride with me some fine night to see our father? Then you will know why the minister keeps his hand over his heart!"

Laughing so shrilly that all the marketplace could hear her, the weird old gentlewoman departed.

By this time, the preliminary prayer had been offered in the meetinghouse and the Reverend Mr. Dimmesdale's voice could be heard as he began his sermon. The meetinghouse was filled to overflowing, so Hester took up a place near the scaffold. It was close enough that she could hear the murmur and flow of the minister's voice, although the words were indistinct.

The minister's voice was like a rich-sounding instrument. The mere tone and cadence of it could carry the listener along. Muffled as the sound was by the church walls, Hester listened intently. The sermon had meaning for her apart from its indistinguishable words. At moments the majestic voice rose in solemn grandeur. At other times, it diminished into a gentleness that soothed. Like music, it breathed passion and pathos into the human heart. But throughout it all, there was an underlying cry of pain. What was it? The complaint of a human heart telling its secret, whether of guilt or sorrow, to the great heart of mankind. It was this profound and continual undertone that gave the clergyman his power.

During the whole sermon, Hester stood statue-like at the foot of the scaffold. There was a magnetism in that spot from which she dated the first hour of her life of shame. There was a sense within her that the whole sphere of her life, both before and after, was connected with this spot. This one point gave her life unity.

Little Pearl, meanwhile, had left her mother's side and was playing about the marketplace. She made the somber crowd cheerful by her erratic and glittering movements. She was like a bird of bright plumage that illuminates a whole tree of dusky foliage by darting to and fro. There was a charm of beauty and eccentricity that shone through her little figure and sparkled with its activity. This made the Puritans who watched her all the more certain that the child was a demon offspring.

At one point the child flew into the midst of a group of sailors, the swarthy-cheeked wild men of the ocean. They gazed wonderingly and admiringly at Pearl, as if a flake of sea foam had taken the shape of a little maid and been given a soul of sea fire.

The shipmaster was so taken with Pearl that he attempted to put his hand on the child's head. Finding it as impossible to touch her as to catch a hummingbird in the air, he took the gold chain from his hat and tossed it to the child. Pearl immediately twined it around her neck and waist so that it became a part of her.

"Your mother is the woman with the scarlet letter," said the shipmaster. "Will you carry a message to her for me?"

"If the message pleases me, I will," answered Pearl.

"Then tell her," he replied, "that I spoke again with the hump-shouldered old doctor. He said that he will bring his friend aboard with him. So your mother need be concerned only with herself and you. Will you tell her this, witch-baby?"

"Mistress Hibbins says my father is the Prince of the Air!" cried Pearl, with her naughty smile. "If you call me that name, I will tell him and he will chase your ship with a storm."

In a zigzag course across the marketplace, the child returned to her mother. There she communicated the captain's message. Hester's strong, calm, enduring spirit almost sank at last. It had been the moment when a passage seemed to open for the minister and herself out of their labyrinth of misery. And now this dark and grim face of inevitable doom showed itself, right in the middle of their path.

And now, at this lowest moment, she was subjected to another trial. There were many people in town from the surrounding countryside. They had heard tales of the letter, but had never actually seen it. They had now gathered around Hester with a rude and boorish intrusiveness.

They dared not come too close, but they encircled her at a short distance and stared. The gang of sailors came to see what people were looking at. They learned the meaning of the letter and thrust their sunburned, desperado-looking faces into the ring. Even the Indians were curious and, gliding through the crowd, fastened their black eyes on Hester's breast. Some of the townspeople, long familiar with the mark of shame, joined the crowd. Hester recognized the group of matrons who had awaited her emergence from the prison door seven years ago. Only the youngest of them—the one who had shown compassion—was not among them. Hester had since made a burial robe for her. Hester was soon to fling aside the burning letter. But, at this final hour, it had strangely kindled a new excitement and interest. In this way, it was made to sear her breast more painfully than at any time since the first day she put it on.

Hester stood in the magic circle of shame where the cunning cruelty of her sentence seemed to have placed her forever. At that same moment, the admirable preacher was looking down from the sacred pulpit on an audience who had given their inmost spirits over to his control. The sainted minister in the church! The woman of the scarlet letter in the marketplace! What mind could possibly have imagined that the same scorching stigma was on them both!

CHAPTER 23

The Revelation
of the Scarlet Letter

The eloquent voice eventually stopped. It had borne the souls of the audience aloft, as on the swelling waves of the sea. There was a momentary silence while the awe-struck listeners gradually returned to themselves. In a moment more, the crowd began to gush forth from the doors of the church.

In the open air, their rapture broke into speech. The street and the marketplace absolutely babbled from side to side with the praise for the minister. Never had man spoken in so wise and so holy a spirit as he spoke this day. Inspiration could be seen descending upon him and filling him with marvelous ideas beyond what he had written. But, beneath it all, had been a certain deep, sad undertone, which could only be interpreted as the natural regret of one who would soon pass away. Yes. Their minister whom they so loved would soon leave them in their tears. It was as if an angel, in his passage to the skies, had shaken his bright wings over the people for an instant. As if that angel, at the same time a shadow and a splendor, had shed down a shower of golden truths upon them.

The Reverend Mr. Dimmesdale had come to a moment in his life more brilliant and full of triumph than any previous one. It was the loftiest pedestal this minister of the purest reputation could achieve. Such was the position the minister occupied in the minds of the people at the close of his Election Sermon. He bowed his head forward on the cushions of the pulpit. Meanwhile, Hester Prynne was standing beside the scaffold with the scarlet letter still burning on her breast.

Now was heard again the clangor of the music and the measured step of the military escort. The procession was to go from the church to the town hall. There a solemn banquet would complete the ceremonies of the day.

The crowd drew back as the procession of magistrates and ministers made its way back through the marketplace. As they made their way, a shout went up. Never, from the soil of New England, had gone up such a shout! Never, on New England soil, had stood a man so honored by his mortal brethren as the preacher!

As the ranks of military men and civil fathers moved onward, all eyes were turned toward the point where the minister was seen approaching. The shout died into a murmur as one portion of the crowd after another got a glimpse of him. How feeble and pale he looked amid all his triumph! The glow, which they had just before seen burning on his cheek, was extinguished, like a flame that sinks down hopelessly among the late-decaying embers. It seemed hardly the face of a man alive, with such a deathlike paleness. It was hardly a man with life in him that tottered on his path so nervelessly.

One of his clerical brethren, the Reverend John Wilson, stepped forward hastily to offer support. The minister tremulously but decidedly repelled the old man's arm. He continued to walk unsteadily forward. And now, he came opposite the weather-darkened scaffold. Next to it stood Hester, holding little Pearl by the hand! And there was the scarlet letter on her breast! Here the minister paused. The music still played the stately and rejoicing march to which the procession moved. It summoned him onward to the festival—but here he paused.

Bellingham had kept an anxious eye on him. The governor now left his place in the procession and approached to give assistance. But there was something in Mr. Dimmesdale's expression that warned the magistrate back. The crowd looked on with awe and wonder. This earthly faintness was, in their view, only another phase of the minister's celestial strength. Most would not have been surprised if he had ascended before their very eyes and faded into the light of heaven.

He turned toward the scaffold and stretched forth his arms.

"Hester," he said, "come here! Come, my little Pearl!"

He had a ghastly look about him. But there was something at once tender and strangely triumphant in it. The child, with a bird-like motion, flew to him and clasped her arms about his knees. Hester Prynne likewise drew near. She moved slowly, as if drawn by inevitable fate, but paused before she reached him. At this instant old Roger Chillingworth thrust himself through the crowd. So dark, disturbed, and evil was his look that he might have risen up from the lower regions, to snatch back his victim from what he was about to do. The old man rushed forward and caught the minister by the arm.

"Madman, stop! What are you doing?" he whispered. "Wave back that woman! Cast off this child! All will be well! Do not blacken your fame and perish in dishonor! I can still save you! Do you want to bring shame on your sacred profession?"

"Ha, tempter! You are too late!" answered the minister with a fearful but firm look. "Your power is not what it was! With God's help, I shall escape you now!"

He again extended his hand to the woman of the scarlet letter.

"Hester Prynne," he cried, "in the name of Him, so terrible and so merciful! In the name of Him, who gives me grace at last to do what I refused to do seven years ago, come to me and wrap me in your strength. Your strength, Hester—but guided by God's will. This miserable and wronged old man is opposing it with all his might! With all his own might and the fiend's might! Come, Hester! Support me up the steps of this scaffold!"

The crowd was in confusion. The men of rank and dignity were so surprised and perplexed by what they saw that they could only stand in silence. They were unable to accept the most obvious explanation but unable to imagine any other. They watched as the minister, leaning on Hester's shoulder and supported by her arm around him, approached the scaffold and ascended its steps. He still held the hand of the sin-born child clasped in his own. Old Roger Chillingworth followed, as one closely connected with the drama of guilt and sorrow.

"Had you searched the whole earth," he said, looking darkly at the clergyman, "there was no place so secret that you could have escaped me—except on this very scaffold!"

"Thanks be to Him who led me here!" answered the minister.

But he trembled and turned to Hester with an expression of doubt and anxiety in his eyes.

"Is this not better," he murmured with a feeble smile, "than what we dreamed of in the forest?"

"I do not know! I do not know!" she hurriedly replied. "Better? Yes, so we may both die, and little Pearl die with us!"

"For you and Pearl, let it be as God shall order," the minister said. "And God is merciful. Let me now do that which He has made plain to me. Hester, I am a dying man. Let me hurry to take my shame upon myself."

Still supported by Hester and still holding little Pearl's hand, the Reverend Mr. Dimmesdale turned to the respected rulers, to the holy ministers, and to the people. All waited, appalled yet overflowing with tearful sympathy. The noontime sun shone down on the clergyman. It gave a distinctness to his figure as he stood out from all the earth to put his plea of guilty at the bar of Eternal Justice.

"People of New England!" he cried. His voice rose over them, solemn and majestic, but always with a tremor through it. "You that have loved me! You that have thought me holy! See me here, the one sinner of the world! At last I stand on the spot where I should have stood seven years ago. Here, with this woman whose arm—whose strength—sustains me at this dreadful moment! Look at the scarlet letter that Hester wears. You have all shuddered at it. Wherever she has walked, it has cast a lurid gleam of awe and horrible repugnance around her. But there stood one in the midst of you at whose mark of sin and infamy you have not shuddered!"

It seemed at this point as if the minister would not have the strength to continue. But he fought back the bodily weakness that threatened to master him. He threw off all assistance and stepped passionately forward a pace before the woman and the child.

"The mark was on him!" he continued with a kind of fierceness. "God's eye saw it! The angels were forever pointing at it! The Devil knew it well, continually touching it with his burning finger! But he hid it slyly from men. He walked among you with appearance of one who was mournful because he was so pure in a sinful world. And now, at the death hour, he stands up before you! He tells you to look at Hester's scarlet letter! He tells you that, with all its mysterious horror, it is but a shadow of what he bears on his own breast—what burns deep and sears his inmost heart! Do any of you question God's judgment on a sinner? Behold! Behold a dreadful witness of that judgment!"

With a convulsive motion he tore away the ministerial robes from his breast. It was revealed!

For an instant, the gaze of the horror-stricken crowd was concentrated on the ghastly miracle. For an instant, the minister stood with a flush of triumph on his face, as one who had won a victory. Then, down he sank upon the scaffold. Hester partly raised him and supported his head against her breast. Old Roger Chillingworth knelt down beside him with a blank, dull expression out of which the life seemed to have departed.

"You have escaped me!" he said repeatedly. "You have escaped me!"

"May God forgive you!" said the minister. "You, too, have deeply sinned!"

He withdrew his eyes from the old man and fixed them on the woman and the child.

"My little Pearl," he said feebly. There was a sweet and gentle smile over his face. With the burden removed, it seemed almost as if he would be playful with the child. "Dear little Pearl, will you kiss me now? You would not in the forest. But now will you?"

Pearl kissed his lips. A spell was broken. Her tears fell upon her father's cheek. They were a pledge that she would grow up amid human joy and sorrow. She would no longer do constant battle with the world. She would be a woman in the world. Toward both her father and her mother, Pearl's errand as a messenger of anguish was fulfilled.

"Hester," said the clergyman, "farewell!"

"Shall we not meet again?" she whispered, bending her face close to his. "Shall we not spend our immortal life together? You look far into eternity with those bright dying eyes! Tell me what you see."

"Hush, Hester," he said solemnly. "The law we broke—the sin here revealed—let these alone be in your thoughts. I fear! It may be that, when we forgot our God—when we violated our reverence for each other's soul, it was from then on vain to hope that we could meet hereafter, in an everlasting and pure reunion. God knows and He is merciful! He has proved his mercy with my suffering. By giving me this burning torture upon my breast! By sending that dark and terrible old man to keep the torture always searing! By bringing me here, to die this death of triumphant shame before the people! Had any of these agonies been lacking, I would have been lost forever! He has brought me to this salvation. Praised be his name! His will be done! Farewell!"

That final word came forth with the minister's expiring breath. The crowd, silent until then, broke out in a strange, deep murmur of awe and wonder. The murmur rolled heavily after the departed spirit.

CHAPTER 24

Conclusion

In the days that followed, there was more than one account of what people had seen on the scaffold.

Most of the spectators testify to having seen on the minister's breast a SCARLET LETTER imprinted on the flesh. There were various explanations for the origin of this letter. Some claim that the Reverend Mr. Dimmesdale inflicted a hideous torture on himself on the very day that Hester Prynne had first worn her badge of shame. Others contend that the stigma was produced by the magic and poisonous drugs of old Roger Chillingworth. Still others affirm that the symbol was the result of the tooth of remorse gnawing from the minister's inmost heart outward. The reader may choose among these theories.

Certain people, however, saw something

quite different. These witnesses deny that there was any mark whatever on the Reverend Mr. Dimmesdale's breast. Nor, according to them did his dying words even remotely imply his slightest connection with Hester Prynne's shame. These highly respectable witnesses contend that the minister chose to die in the arms of a fallen woman to show the world that we are all sinners—even the most pure among us. And in this way, he wished to show us by his example that the attainment of purity of reputation here on earth is as nothing when compared to the Infinite Purity of the Mercy that looks down on us from above. This version of Mr. Dimmesdale's story is an example of the stubborn devotion with which a man's friends will sometimes uphold his character. This blind devotion continues even when there is proof—proof as clear as the midday sunshine on the scarlet letter—that establishes him as a false and sin-stained creature of the dust.

There are many morals one could draw from the poor minister's miserable experience. But we mention here only this one: "Be true! Show freely to the world, if not your worst, at least some hint by which the worst may be inferred!"

After Mr. Dimmesdale's death, a most remarkable change took place in the appearance of old Roger Chillingworth. All his strength and energy—all his vital and intellectual force—seemed to desert him. He positively withered up, like an uprooted weed that lies wilting in the sun. He shriveled away and almost vanished from mortal sight. This unhappy man had made revenge the very principle of his life. When there was no more devil's work on earth for him to do, the unhumanized mortal could only return to his master.

Old Roger Chillingworth died within the year. In his last will and testament, he left a large amount of property, both in America and in England, to little Pearl.

So Pearl—the elf-child, the demon off-spring—became the richest heiress of her day in the New World. Not surprisingly, this significantly changed how the public viewed her. Had Pearl and her mother remained in the colony until the child was ready to marry, she could have married into the most devout Puritan family in Boston if she wished.

However, not long after the physician's death, the wearer of the scarlet letter disappeared, and Pearl along with her. Now and then a vague report of their whereabouts would find its way across the sea. But no definite news of them was received. The story of the scarlet letter grew into legend. Its spell still shrouded the scaffold where the poor minister had died, as well as the empty cottage by the seashore where Hester had lived. Near the cottage, one afternoon, some children were at play. They saw a tall woman in a gray robe approach the cottage door. In all those years it had not once been opened. The woman either unlocked it or the decayed wood gave way—or perhaps, she glided shadowlike through it—and went in.

On the threshold she paused and turned partly around. Perhaps the idea of entering, all alone and so changed, this home of her former life was more dreary than she could bear. But her hesitation was only for an instant—though long enough to display a scarlet letter on her breast.

Hester Prynne had returned and taken up her long-forsaken shame. But where was little Pearl? If still alive, she would by now have been a young woman. No one knew or ever learned with certainty whether the elf-child had gone to an early grave—or whether her wild, rich nature had been subdued and made capable of a woman's gentle happiness. But throughout the remainder of Hester's life there were indications that she was the object of love and interest of someone who lived in a foreign land. Letters came. They were sealed with a family coat of arms not known in the New World. In the cottage were articles of comfort and luxury. Hester never cared to use these, but they were clearly gifts that had been lovingly imagined for her. There were also little ornaments and beautiful tokens of a continual remembrance from a fond heart. Once, Hester was seen embroidering a baby garment. Its golden decoration was of such lavish richness that no infant in the somber New England community would have been seen in it.

In short, the gossips of that day believed that Pearl was not only alive, but married and happy. In addition, she was mindful of her mother and would joyfully have entertained that sad and lonely woman by her fireside.

But there was a more real life for Hester Prynne here, in New England, than in that unknown region where Pearl had found a home. Here had been her sin; here, her sorrow; and here was yet to be her penitence. She had returned of her own free will. And she had resumed of her own free will the symbol that has cast its dusky glow over this dark tale. Never afterward did she remove it. It ceased to be a stigma that attracted the world's scorn and bitterness. Instead, it became something to be sorrowed over and looked upon with awe and reverence.

People brought her all their sorrows and confusions. They sought her counsel, as one who had herself gone through a mighty trouble. Women, especially, came to Hester's cottage. They brought their recurring trials, their wounded, wasted, misplaced, or sinful passion. They brought the dreary burden of a heart unsatisfied because it was unvalued and unwanted. Hester comforted and counseled them. She assured them, too, as she believed, that at some time the world would be a better place. In some brighter time, a new truth would be revealed. It would establish the whole relation between man and woman on a surer ground of mutual happiness.

Earlier in her life, Hester had vainly imagined that she herself might be the one destined to bring this new truth to the world. But she had since realized that such a messenger could not be bowed down with shame or burdened with a life-long sorrow. The angel of the coming revelation must indeed be a woman, but one lofty and pure and wise. Such a woman would lead us, not through grief but through joy, to a new relation. She would show us, through a life successfully lived, how sacred love should make us happy.

So said Hester Prynne, and glanced her sad eyes downward at the scarlet letter. After many, many years, a new grave was dug in the burial ground at King's Chapel. It was dug near an old and sunken grave. There was a space between the two graves, as if the dust of the two sleepers had no right to mingle. But one tombstone served for both. On this simple slab of slate was chiseled a family shield. Beneath the shield were carved words that might serve to close our now concluded legend:

"On a background of black, the letter A in red"

Afterword

About the Author

Nathaniel Hawthorne was forty-five years old when he wrote *The Scarlet Letter*. The book sold well. It did not, however, bring Hawthorne as much financial reward as it might have. But financial difficulties were nothing new to the author.

Hawthorne's father was a sea captain. While on a voyage to South America in 1808, the captain died of yellow fever. Hawthorne was four years old. He and his mother and two sisters lived in Salem, Massachusetts. The captain's death left the family with very little money. As a result, his mother was forced to give up their house and move the family in with her relatives.

As a young boy, Hawthorne enjoyed taking solitary walks around Salem. When he was fifteen, his mother moved the family to Sebago

Lake in Maine. There they lived with a great-uncle. In the wilderness around the lake, Hawthorne continued his habit of taking long walks. Throughout his youth, he kept a journal in which he wrote about his wanderings and adventures. But, in spite of the pleasure he got from the walks, he did not find his boyhood particularly joyful. Years later, he wrote to a friend of the "gloom and chill of my early life."

While the family was living in Maine, the great-uncle decided that he would pay for Hawthorne to go to Bowdoin College. Therefore, after a year at Sebago Lake, the family moved back to Salem so that Hawthorne could prepare for college. In 1821, at the age of seventeen, Hawthorne enrolled at Bowdoin. By this time, he had decided he wanted to be a writer. In a letter to his mother, he said, "I do not want to be a doctor and live by men's diseases, nor a minister and live by their sins, nor a lawyer and live by their quarrels. So I do not see that there is anything left for me but to be an author. How would you like some day to see a whole shelf full of books written by your son . . . ?"

After graduating from Bowdoin in 1825, Hawthorne returned to his mother's home in Salem, where he lived with her and his two sisters for the next twelve years. His mother had begun to withdraw from society shortly after her husband's death. By the time Hawthorne moved back after college, she was living in seclusion. She took her meals in her room and seldom left the house. He referred to his mother's house as "Castle Dismal."

Hawthorne spent much of his time reading, writing, and studying. In 1828, he published the novel *Fanshawe* anonymously and at his own expense. It did not sell well, and he soon decided he was ashamed of it. He burned all of the unsold copies. He did get a few stories published in these years, but the family continued to struggle financially.

In 1838, he met Sophia Peabody and a year later became engaged to her. However, he still was not making much money and did not feel he could afford to marry her. Through the help of influential friends, he got a job as a measurer of salt and coal at the Custom House in Boston. But he found the work dull and tiring and he was unhappy that it did not leave him with enough energy to write. After holding the position for two years, he resigned in 1841. After that, he spent a few months living and working in an experimental utopian community called Brook Farm. Here, too, he found the work responsibilities left him too tired to write, so he left.

In 1842, he reached an agreement with a magazine to pay him for his writing. He still was not earning much, but he and Sophia decided to marry anyway. In July of that year, right after the wedding, the couple moved to Concord, Massachusetts. Two years later, their first daughter, Una, was born. The family's financial troubles continued. As a result, they moved back to his mother's house in Salem in 1845. Eventually, again with the help of influential friends, Hawthorne was appointed surveyor and inspector for the Custom House at Salem. He held the position for three years. In June of 1849, as a result of the political maneuverings of a legislator named Charles Upham, he was fired from the job. Supposedly, when he arrived home and told Sophia of his dismissal, she said cheerfully, "Now you can write your book."

A few weeks later, Hawthorne's mother died. Hawthorne wrote in his journal that there had "been, ever since my boyhood, a sort of coldness . . . between us." However, in the same journal entry, he wrote that, as he entered the room where she lay dying, "I did not expect to be much moved . . . but I was moved to kneel down . . . and take her hand. . . . I found the tears gathering in my eyes. . . . For a few moments, I shook with sobs. For a long time, I knelt there, holding her hand; and surely, it is the darkest hour I ever lived."

Shortly after his mother's death, Hawthorne began work on a novel. Six months later, on February 3, 1850, Hawthorne completed *The Scarlet Letter*.

Although the novel is not autobiographical,

some elements of Hawthorne's family may have given him ideas for the story. Hawthorne's great-great-great-grandfather was raised in England. His name was William Hathorne. (Nathaniel Hawthorne added the *w* to his name when he was a young man, in order to make the spelling consistent with the pronunciation.) At the age of twenty-one, William converted to Puritanism. A couple of years later, about 1630, he left England for the new Massachusetts Bay Colony in America. By 1636, he was settled in Salem and quickly became a prominent citizen. He believed that God had placed him on earth for the purpose of seeing that his neighbors lived righteous and God-fearing lives. As a magistrate, he ordered that Quakers be arrested, whipped, and banished for their religious practices. In 1659, he influenced the court in Boston to hang two men for being Quakers.

Nathaniel's great-great grandfather, John Hathorne, also became a magistrate. John was as much a fanatic as his father. But instead of persecuting Quakers, he concentrated on witches. In 1692, he and another judge conducted hearings that resulted in the trial of three women for witchcraft. Over the next few months, he sent almost one hundred people to jail to await trial for witchcraft. In the end, nineteen of them were convicted and hanged and one was tortured to death.

In *The Scarlet Letter,* it is clear that

Hawthorne disapproves of the "harshly strict and severe" rules and punishments of Puritan society. And he may well have been thinking of his own ancestors when he wrote:

> **Maybe a Quaker was to be beaten and chased out of town and into the wilderness for his religious beliefs. Or possibly some poor woman condemned as a witch was to die on the gallows. No matter what the case, the criminal being punished could expect no sympathy from the bystanders, no matter how extreme the punishment.**

When Hawthorne created the character of Hester Prynne, he may have had his mother's forty years of isolation in mind. He frequently reminds us that Hester is constantly separated from the rest of society. As Hawthorne says in Chapter 2, the letter "had the effect of a spell, taking her out of the ordinary relations with humanity and enclosing her in a sphere by herself."

Hawthorne's daughter Una may have been the model for the elf-child Pearl. Una is said to have been a fascinating but very difficult child. When his daughter was five, Hawthorne wrote the following about her in his journal: "There is something that almost frightens me about the child—I know not whether elfish or angelic, but, at all events, supernatural." He also wrote that she sometimes seemed "a spirit strangely mingling good and evil."

Sophia may have influenced Hawthorne's ideas for the novel as well. She was a strong-minded, resourceful, and supportive wife. She was an artist. During the time Hawthorne was writing *The Scarlet Letter,* she helped support the family by painting fire screens and lampshades that were sold in Boston. She may also have influenced his ideas about the role of women in society. In Chapter 13, we are told that Hester believes the role of women must be improved. "The first step toward improvement would be to tear the whole system down and build it up anew. Then, the very nature of man must be essentially modified before woman would be allowed to assume what would seem like a fair and suitable position in the world." It is also hard to imagine that, if Hawthorne had remained an isolated bachelor, he would have been able to write a story about a woman as strong, as passionate, and as forward thinking as Hester Prynne.

In the two years after Hawthorne completed *The Scarlet Letter*, he published two more novels—*The House of the Seven Gables* and *The Blithedale Romance*—as well as collections of short writings. In 1852, he bought a house in Concord, Massachusetts. He named it "The Wayside." At the age of forty-seven, Hawthorne moved his wife and three children into their first permanent home. That same year, he wrote *The*

Life of Franklin Pierce. Franklin Pierce had been a classmate and friend at Bowdoin College. Pierce was running for president of the United States and this book was his campaign biography. When Pierce became president, he rewarded Hawthorne by appointing him United States Consul at Liverpool, England. The Hawthornes remained in England from 1853 until 1857. The family then moved to Italy for two years. In 1859, Hawthorne finished the manuscript for his final complete novel *The Marble Faun.* In June of 1860, the family returned to their house in Concord.

Within a year, Hawthorne's health began to fail. He was able to write less and less. In May of 1864, he began a tour of the White Mountains in New Hampshire with his old friend Franklin Pierce. During the trip, he died in his sleep on May 19, in Plymouth, New Hampshire. He left behind Sophia and his three children—Una, Julian, and Rose. He was sixty years old.

About the Book

In the final chapter of *The Scarlet Letter* Hawthorne writes:

> There are many morals one could draw from the poor minister's miserable experience. But we mention here only this one: "Be true! Show freely to the world, if not your worst, at least some hint by which the worst may be inferred!"

This seems like a very strange lesson. Is Hawthorne really telling us to show people our worst qualities, so they will be able to figure out how bad we truly are? On its face, this does not seem like very good advice. But if we look closely at the stories of Arthur Dimmesdale and Hester Prynne, we can see the blessings of "being true"—and the horror of living with falsehood.

In *The Scarlet Letter*, Hawthorne makes it clear that being true is difficult. From the start of the novel, Dimmesdale wants to reveal his worst secret—that he is the father of Hester's child. But the minister lacks the courage to do so. Instead, he tries to get Hester to speak for him. In Chapter 3, when Hester is standing on the scaffold, Dimmesdale begs her to reveal the name of her lover—his own name:

I urge you to speak out the name of your fellow sinner. . . . Heaven has granted you the opportunity to work out an open triumph over evil within yourself. Do not deny him the same chance, for perhaps he does not have the courage to grasp the opportunity himself.

But Hester refuses to do Dimmesdale's moral duty for him. And instead of stepping forward and of confessing, Dimmesdale seals the truth within his heart and hides it from the world: "'She will not speak!' murmured Mr. Dimmesdale, his hand upon his heart." This is the start of his moral downfall.

Unlike Dimmesdale, Hester does have the courage to be true. Instead of trying to hide her adulterer's symbol from the world, she has made it into a bold, gorgeous thing, bright red and "embroidered with . . . extravagance." Through her scarlet letter, she literally shows her worst "freely to the world." Wearing it, she emerges from the prison and walks toward the scaffold with "a proud smile on her lips . . ."

Despite her external boldness, Hester suffers deeply. As she walks from the prison to the scaffold, "she felt agony with every footstep, as if her heart had been flung into the street for everyone in the crowd to scorn and trample on." In the years that follow, she continues to suffer for her honesty. "Everyone she came in contact with . . . scorned and insulted her, either openly or with subtle looks." Her truthfulness means that she can never escape the world's scorn. "Hester always suffered dreadful agony when she felt a human eye on the symbol." Meanwhile, dishonest Dimmesdale continues to live the life of an upright, respected man, loved and admired by everybody.

Why does Hawthorne advise us to show our worst if doing so will cause us such pain? A look at Dimmesdale's life answers the question. Unlike Hester, who suffers because people know the truth about her, Dimmesdale suffers because people do *not* know the truth about him. Every moment of his life, he is tormented by his own hypocrisy. His status as a man of God in the community makes his situation all the more agonizing. He sincerely loves God and the truth, but he is too cowardly to live according to his convictions. With every day, his hatred of his own flawed self grows deeper.

In contrast, once Hester has shown the world her worst, life gradually becomes more bearable. Although she is isolated from society, "as if she inhabited another sphere," she is not isolated from humanity. Her scarlet letter brings her closer to the human spirit. At times she feels as if "she possessed a new sense, a new awareness of others." Her own suffering has given her a deep sense of compassion for others. Over the years, her charitable work earns her "a reputation as one who tirelessly helped the poor, the sick, the needy. . . . She was a wellspring of human tenderness. The world now saw her as a Sister of Mercy." Even thought Hester does not have social interactions in the usual sense, she is very much connected to the world around her.

For Dimmesdale, his soul's anguish becomes his only real existence. The falsehood of his life "steals the substance out of the realities around" him. It becomes increasingly difficult for the minister to trust his own perceptions—to distinguish between what is actual and what is imaginary. We observe this confusion as we watch his relationship with Roger Chillingworth develop. Many of the townspeople view Chillingworth with revulsion and suspicion: "(It) became the opinion of many that Reverend Arthur Dimmesdale was haunted either by Satan or by Satan's emissary in the appearance of old Roger Chillingworth." At times the minister wonders about the doctor, but his own deep sense of guilt blinds him:

> He sometimes looked with fearful suspicion—even, at times, with horror and the bitterness of hatred—on the misshapen old physician. But he could find no cause for his feelings in the old man's words or actions, so he would conclude they must come from the evil secret that lay within his own heart.

For Dimmesdale, the whole universe has become false. As a result, he believes that Chillingworth is his friend when, in fact, the physician is a fiend who torments him.

Eventually, Dimmesdale becomes so paralyzed by the falseness of his life that he cannot think for himself. When Hester meets him in the forest and tells him Chillingworth's real identity, Dimmesdale is helpless. He says, "Think for me, Hester! You are strong. Decide for me!" A moment later, he asks, "Should I lie down again on these withered leaves and die at once? Be strong for me. Advise me what to do!" Hester suggests that he go back to Europe, but he says, "I am powerless to go." He continues, "I must die here. There is not the strength or courage left in me to venture into the strange, difficult world alone!"

As these two people's lives demonstrates, it takes strength and courage to be true. Dimmesdale lacks those qualities. He chooses to live with admiration that he knows is unearned rather than with scorn that would be genuine. The result is that his life becomes a nightmare of hypocrisy and self-loathing. When he does, finally, reveal his worst to the world, he is too much weakened to survive the experience. He dies.

Hester, by contrast, chooses to be true. She has the strength and courage to show the world her worst. Her honesty has a price; she is initially scorned in the eyes of the world. But truthfulness eventually earns the world's genuine respect. The scarlet letter "ceased to be a stigma that attracted the world's scorn and bitterness. Instead it became . . . looked upon with awe and reverence."

> **There are many morals one could draw from the poor minister's miserable experience. But we mention here only this one: "Be true! Show freely to the world, if not your worst, at least some hint by which the worst may be inferred!"**

It seems that what Hawthorne means is this: Only by being genuine can we be our best selves. When we deny our soul's truth, as Dimmesdale did, we run the risk of destroying ourselves. Hawthorne suggests that it is better to take responsibility for our actions, even when it means showing the world our worst. Then, like Hester, we can be our best.